Challenge a Scarecrow

Dorothy Bodoin

A Wings ePress, Inc.
Cozy Mystery Novel

Wings ePress, Inc.

Edited by: Jeanne Smith
Copy Edited by: Christie Kraemer
Executive Editor: Jeanne Smith
Cover Artist: Trisha FitzGerald-Jung

All rights reserved

Wings ePress Books
www.wingsepress.com

Copyright © 2020 by: Dorothy Bodoin
ISBN-13: 978-1-61309-587-4
ISBN-10: 1-61309-587-2

Published In the United States Of America

Wings ePress Inc.
3000 N. Rock Road
Newton, KS 67114

What They Are Saying About

Challenge a Scarecrow

Challenge A Scarecrow by Dorothy Bodoin is a great addition to the Foxglove Corners series.

Are you one of those people who's afraid of clowns? Well, get ready for scarecrows. They can be frightening, too, and deadly.

Our heroine, Jennet Ferguson, attends an annual Apple Fair where she purchases a miniature Victorian house to give to the town's librarian, Miss Eidt. The reception of the gift is a surprise and leads to plenty of suspense and eventually to a dozen eerie scarecrows standing behind the real-life version of the little house.

In the meantime, Jennet meets a woman who believes she's brought her deceased dog back to life. Is the woman crazy or is she onto something?

This is a unique story that I highly recommend. If you're looking for something different to read, look no more. This one will keep you on the edge of your seat.

Five Stars.

Marja McGraw
author of the Sandi Webster mysteries

Dedication

Dedicated to Jeanne Smith,
Executive Editor of Wings ePress,
the best editor an author could have
and a good friend as well.

* * *

One

The apple was magnificent: plump and practically irresistible with its glossy coat of nut-studded caramel. Truly heaven on a stick. I took a great bite and hoped my front teeth were still in their proper place.

It tasted as good as it looked, definitely a McIntosh. But darn it all. Now my hand was sticky, even though I hadn't touched the caramel.

Annica's apple earrings sparkled in the sunlight amid strands of red-gold hair. Her caramel apple was already half gone. "Super delicious," she said. "Do you remember reading about the lady who ate an apple just like this and dropped down dead?"

I took a second bite. "No. Are you talking about a story?"

"A *true* story. The apple was poisoned. She was a high school English teacher."

I studied her expression, searching for a tell-tale, teasing gleam in her eyes. Annica, the girl I'd met at the antique shop, Past Perfect, where she worked briefly, had excelled in spinning macabre tales about her wares. Rings that dispensed poison and choker necklaces that literally melded to the hapless wearer's throat. She had a thousand stories. I didn't believe one of them.

"It's true," she said. "I swear it."

"When did this happen?"

"Here in Maple Creek, one year at the Apple Fair. Don't worry. They caught the poisoner."

"Well..." Offhand, I couldn't think of a suitable response. Fortunately, Annica's tale didn't diminish my pleasure in eating the caramel apple. Nothing could do that on this glorious autumn afternoon.

It was the first day of Maple Creek's annual Apple Fair. The trees were at the peak of their brilliant fall color with leaves ranging from pale yellow to deep crimson. Clouds floated in a cerulean sky. They were so white and puffy they might have been made of cotton candy. Which had inspired our purchases of marshmallow-nut fudge, along with bushels of rosy McIntosh apples from the Brightwater Cider Mill.

Still thinking of apples, I said, "That sounds like a fairy tale. Wasn't it Snow White's wicked stepmother who tried to kill her with a poisoned apple?"

"Yes, the wicked queen who wanted to be the fairest in the land. Fairy tales are scary."

"And the moral of the story is: Beware of poisoned apples?"

"Or beware of envious women."

"We don't have to worry about poison or wicked women today," I said.

I tossed the apple core into the nearest receptacle and scanned the crowds streaming from one attraction to the next.

"What would you like to look at now?" I asked

"The crafts. There's a booth in the park. I'd love to have an apple maid doll."

"A doll?"

A faint blush stole over her face. "A little one. Like a figurine. For a souvenir."

"Crafts it is then," I said.

Dolls weren't on my 'favorites' list, but I'd been looking forward to finding a new wreath for my front door, one with pumpkins or gourds, orange florals, and a long trailing ribbon.

The heart of the Maple Creek Apple Fair was its park, renowned for the many fountains that provided continuous background music of falling water. Interspersed with trees, meticulously tended flower beds were bursting with brilliant fall color, and bright balloons tied to low-hanging branches floated languidly in the mild breeze. The booths, set up in the center of the park, offered all kinds of seasonal treats, including caramel apples, apple-themed baked goods, and crafts.

We found the apple maid dolls at the first booth we came to, set up near one of the fountains with an angel or fairy—it was difficult to know which—dispensing water from a horn. The dolls were all sizes, mostly clothed in red or green, and always holding an apple or wearing jewelry fashioned in imitation of one. The doll Annica chose wore a coronet of tiny apples on her long auburn hair and earrings, miniatures of the ones Annica wore.

The woman in charge of the booth fit my picture of Snow White's wicked stepmother. She seemed regal and haughty, and her hair was so black it had blue lights. She didn't appear to be remotely interested in promoting her crafts. She took Annica's money, wrapped the doll in white tissue paper, and handed it over, all with a baffling lack of enthusiasm.

Annica tucked her doll in her tote bag. "I wonder if the real Apple Maid is on duty today."

"She's supposed to wander through the Fair, handing out apples and posing for pictures," I said. "We're bound to run into her if we keep walking. Oh...look!"

My gaze rested on a miniature house set amid the apple dolls. It was the only one in sight. Dark brown in color and boasting five gables and a wraparound porch, it appeared as if every light in the house was burning. Unadorned black wreaths hung from every window and the overall effect was depressing. No, spooky was a better way to describe it.

The house sat in a square of crimson maple leaves carved in thin wood. They were so realistic that you could imagine the crunching sound they'd make when you tread on them.

Take me, the house seemed to beg. *So what if I cost more than anything else you bought today? Payday is next Friday.*

"I'm going to buy it," I said.

"Yes!" Annica reached out to run her fingers along the bed of maple leaves. I half expected them to move. "It'll be a neat decoration for Halloween. You can put it on your mantel."

"I could, but it's going to be a gift."

The regal woman turned her attention to us. "A good choice. It's the only one I have."

"Did you sell out of them already?" Annica asked.

"I meant that's the only one the craftsman made."

"I'll take it," I said. Turning to Annica, I added, "I'm going to give it to Miss Eidt for her Gothic Nook."

Our librarian, Elizabeth Eidt, had lived with her family in an old white Victorian on Park Street. Years later, when she was alone, she donated the house to the town of Foxglove Corners to use as a library, along with many books from her own collection, and moved to a small, one-story bungalow. Recently, she had created a nook in the library consisting mostly of paperback Gothic novels rescued from yard and estate sales.

Miss Eidt had furnished the Gothic Nook with antique chairs, tables, and lamps, going so far as to set out dishes of candy for readers who wanted to escape into a Gothic world for a few hours. The miniature house would be perfect on her prized Duncan Phyfe table.

"Miss Eidt likes doll houses," Annica pointed out, referring to the replica of the library which she brought out of storage and decorated for different seasons. "But big ones. Why do you think she'd like a miniature like this?"

I reached for my credit card, which I'd have to use as I'd already spent most of my cash. The little house was expensive at seventy-five dollars, but I didn't hesitate. "It's a way to thank her for all the help she's given me."

"Hey, Jennet!"

Jennifer and Molly, my young friends who lived on Sagramore Lake Road, appeared in front of us, seemingly dropping out of thin air.

Glowing with health and energy, they wore denim shorts and Apple Fair shirts from the previous year. They were almost grown up, but their long ponytails made them look younger than their years. They were high school sophomores.

I noticed their hands were empty. "Are you girls enjoying the Fair?"

"It's fun but we're on a mission," Jennifer said.

Molly took up the story. "Did you see a small black collie? We're trying to catch her. She came this way."

I glanced at Annica who shook her head.

"Maybe she got away from her owner who's looking for her right now," I said.

Molly shook her head. "We don't think so. She isn't wearing a collar."

"Will you help us?" Jennifer asked. "I mean, that's what you do."

In truth, I taught English at Marston High School, but I also belonged to the Lakeville Collie Rescue League. Jennifer was right. I didn't go about my days searching for a collie in distress, but if I stumbled over one—in some cases literally—I would do everything in my power to rescue her or him.

Annica reached for my purchase. "I'll take our stuff to the car and wait for you back here."

I guessed I'd been recruited. "Okay," I said. "Which way?"

Molly pointed beyond the booth and the merrily splashing fairy-angel fountain. "Straight ahead," she said.

Two

Straight ahead, I saw the mermaid fountain and a booth well-stocked with caramel apples, cider sold by the cup and gallon, and white boxes exactly the size for pies.

Here, we found the stray collie standing over a pie on the ground, devouring it in great gulps. She was a tricolor, small and compact in build, with an unkempt coat. Her ribs were prominent, telling a tale of malnourishment. Probably, she didn't have an owner.

A rosy-cheeked woman in denim and blue gingham berated her in a loud screechy voice.

"Uh-oh," Jennifer said.

Rosy Cheeks halted her tirade to address Jennifer. "Is this your dog, Miss? If it is, you owe me ten dollars. She knocked that box down from the counter with her paw and tore into it like a wolf."

The pie was almost gone, the collie oblivious of the angry human.

"We were trying to catch her to..." Jennifer broke off with a helpless look at Molly.

"To return her to her owner," Molly said.

"It's a little late for my pie, isn't it?"

Having licked the box clean of crumbs, the collie turned back to the stacks of pies on the counter and began sniffing them.

"Ugly black scarecrow." The woman slammed her fist on the counter. "Get!" Unfazed, the collie continued her perusal of the pies.

"Get her out of here!" Rosy Cheeks demanded.

Good grief. Why were these Fair workers so unpleasant?

Jennifer laid her hand on the collie's neck where a collar would have been. The dog wrenched out of her reach but didn't growl or bare her teeth. On the contrary, she wagged her tail, albeit slowly.

"Did you bring any treats with you today, Jennet?" Molly asked.

"Yes, I always do, but they're in my car. I have a spare collar and leash there, too."

The woman began to tap numbers on her cell phone. "Animal Control will deal with this one."

"Wait!" I opened my shoulder bag. She'd said her pies cost ten dollars. Thinking to mollify her, I pulled out two five-dollar bills, the last of the cash I'd brought with me. I had some change in my coin purse, though, quite a few quarters. Quickly, I counted.

"Do you have anything for a dollar and seventy-five cents?" I asked.

She handed over a small box, frowning at the change I dropped into her hand. "A bear claw with Michigan apple filling."

"That'll do."

I handed the box to Jennifer. Our little pie thief gave a piteous whine and licked her chops.

"Break them into little pieces," I said. "We'll lure her back to my car."

Then Sue Appleton, president of the Lakeville Collie Rescue League, would take charge of the collie and find her owner. If that proved impossible, Sue would find her a new home.

Would my pastry ploy work?

Jennifer opened the box and held it well away from the collie's mouth. Delicious smells of apple and cinnamon drifted out into the air. The collie licked her chops again. Jennifer broke off a tiny piece of the claw and held it in front of the dog's long nose while Molly and I began walking slowly toward the craft booth.

"That smells *so* good," Molly said.

Annica was waiting for us at the crafts booth. "I see you found her."

"Now, we have to get her to the car."

All the way, Molly and Jennifer took turns giving the collie a bite of the pastry to show her what delights waited for her if she would just follow us.

She did. I breathed a sigh of relief as Jennifer threw the last piece in the back seat of my Ford Focus. The collie leaped in after it.

"Do you want to go back to the Fair, Jennet?" Molly asked. "We can sit with the dog if you do."

"Thanks, but I'm ready to go home," I said.

Home to my beloved Foxglove Corners with a bushel of McIntosh apples, a miniature spooky house, and no autumn wreath for my door.

Oh, well. Rescuing collies took precedence over decorations and I could return to the Fair the next day, if I so desired.

~ * ~

When I reached Jonquil Lane, I drove past my house, satisfied that it looked peaceful and quiet in its surround of fading flowers and falling leaves. The sun shone on the stained-glass window between the twin turrets, and I longed to unwind in my rocker with a cup of hot tea.

Not yet, though.

I couldn't bring the tricolor stray inside to mingle with my own seven collies until she'd been vetted. She? The tricolor needed a name. Any name but Scarecrow. Licorice? No.

Velvet? The word dropped into my mind and instantly felt right. When she was groomed, her coat would be like black velvet.

She was sitting in the back seat of the Focus, her hunger abated with the bear claw, watching the scenery go by. Woods and the gloomy abandoned construction of falling-apart French chateau style houses swam by in a light haze. Where Jonquil Lane ended at Squill Lane, I turned right and drove on to Sue's horse ranch. She would be expecting us as I'd called her before leaving the Fair.

As I led Velvet up to the ranch house, I paused, mesmerized by the explosion of color all around me. Leaves turned to gold and scarlet, a respectable amount of green remaining, a sky the rich blue of cornflowers, and graceful horses grazing behind the corral—all of this beauty crying out to be captured by an artist.

From inside the house, Sue's dogs were barking, either a welcome or a warning.

Who could tell? She opened the door and grabbed the collar of Bluebell, her merle who insisted on staying by her side. The others, more obedient, had retreated at her command.

In spite of her countrywoman's outfit of blue jeans and white cotton, Sue reinforced the color scheme with a scarlet band in her strawberry blonde hair and a silk scarf patterned with red poppies knotted around her neck.

"This must be our little apple girl," she said, offering her palm to Velvet to sniff.

The barking and the sight of Bluebell combined to intimidate Velvet. She held her ears flat against her head, and her tail disappeared between her hind legs.

"She's really not timid," I said. "The pie maker was a witch of a woman, but Velvet stood up to her. She stole a pie and was ready to help herself to another one."

"She wasn't wearing a collar? Doctor Foster will check to see if she's microchipped. If not, we'll advertise for her owner."

"When she's bathed and fattened up a bit, she'll be a beauty," I said. "A black beauty."

"And she's young. So no candidate for Brent's home for geriatric collies."

Our friend, the incomparable huntsman and perennial bachelor, Brent Fowler, had recently opened a house for older collies whose hope of finding a new home had long since passed. Presided over by Lila and Letty Woodville, who had managed the Foxglove Corners Animal Shelter, the place was already a resounding success.

But Velvet would undoubtedly find a forever home of her own. If her owners couldn't be located.

"Either her people brought her to the Fair and abandoned her, or she wandered in by herself," I said.

Sue nodded. "Lured by the smell of food."

"And maybe people at the Fair fed her tidbits," I said, "But she was still hungry. She's hungry now."

"Let me settle her in the barn with some kibble," she added. "I already called Alice for an appointment."

She took Velvet's leash from me. "Make yourself at home, Jennet. When I come back, have a glass of cider with me. I visited the cider mill yesterday. Brightwater cider is the best I ever tasted."

Cold cider or hot tea. Either one was welcome, but—

"Can I have a raincheck?" I asked. "I've been away all day. I have seven collies and a husband to take care of."

In that order.

"Sure," she said. "Whenever you have time."

Three

I had been a single woman with one collie when I fell in love with the green Victorian farmhouse on Jonquil Lane. Built on ten acres of land and painted mint green, my favorite color, it had a stained-glass window between double gables and a wide front porch. The house possessed all the gingerbread ornamentation I could desire.

It was my dream house, and it became a home when I married my true love, Deputy Sheriff Crane Ferguson, and, over time, added six rescue collies to the household.

Crane was already home, and the dogs, knowing I was near, were barking. Camille, my neighbor and aunt by marriage, lived in the yellow Victorian house across the lane. She had taken care of them while I was at the Apple Fair, as she did during the week.

I was incredibly lucky in my marriage, in Camille and my other friends, and in my life. Also in my career...most of the time. But it was still Saturday and my first class was hours away.

Leaving the apples in the trunk, I took the miniature house and walked up to the side door which led to the kitchen. I ran into an avalanche of leaping, yipping collies who thought I'd abandoned them. Halley, Candy, Gemmy, Raven, Sky, Star, and Misty. My own collies had never known hunger in my care, nor heard words that weren't kind and loving. I dispensed individual pats on the head to each one.

Crane sat at the oak table drinking a cup of coffee and poring over a map. A delicious aroma emanated from the oven. Pizza.

"Did you have a good time at the Fair, honey?" he asked.

I set the little house on the counter. "Pretty good. I bought two bushels of apples and a gift for Miss Eidt."

He smiled. "That looks like something Lucy would like."

He referred to our good friend, Lucy Hazen, who lived in an atmospheric house known as Dark Gables where she wrote horror novels slanted toward teen-aged readers.

I laid my hand on his shoulder and kissed his cheek. "That's true, but I can also see it in Miss Eidt's Gothic Nook."

As I spoke, I realized that Crane had yet to see the library's newest innovation.

"Will you bring the apples in from the car?" I asked. "We'll have pies and all things apple for the foreseeable future."

"Sure thing. There's a pizza for dinner. I didn't trust myself to make a salad."

"I'll do it," I said. "And—drum roll—I rescued a collie today."

I told him how we'd lured Velvet into the car with bear claw bites after she'd wolfed down an entire pie. "She's with Sue now. I'd say it was a good day. Why are you looking at the map?"

"Scouting out vacation spots. How would you like to go on a short fall trip?"

"I'd love it!" The following instant reality tapped me on the head. "But it would have to coincide with a school vacation. Are you thinking of Thanksgiving?"

"Maybe sooner than that. A long weekend. Maybe you could take a sick day."

"A personal business day," I said. "Yes, that would work. If you can get the time off. Where would we go?"

"Up north? To Mackinac Island, before they close down for the winter?"

"It sounds like heaven," I said.

Summer had come and gone, busy and relaxing when it wasn't hectic. We hadn't taken a vacation. In fact, we hadn't been anywhere together since our honeymoon. If only we could take our seven collies with us. But once again, Camille would step in for us. And the dogs would keep one another company in their own home.

Reality rose its head again. "The problem with taking a day off is that my bad classes will run amok. Then they'll be harder to manage the next day."

I had a different schedule this year: two English Literature classes, a subject I hadn't taught before with older students, mostly seniors, and a group of freshmen who prided themselves on their talent for making trouble.

Well, I'd survive. Who doesn't love a challenge?

"I'll start on that salad," I said, and began to gather ingredients.

Having something happy to look forward to was a perfect ending to a day that had been, on the whole, enjoyable.

~ * ~

The weekend had flown by as if warp speed had taken it over. On Monday morning, I sent Crane off to patrol the roads of Foxglove Corners after a hearty breakfast. Then, packing school books and lunch, I set off to pick up my longtime friend and fellow teacher, Leonora. We took turns driving the hour-long distance to and from school in Oakpoint.

Leonora deposited her books in the back seat of the Focus and pushed back the strands of long blonde hair that had fallen forward in her face. As always she looked fresh and pretty, only a few of the qualities which made her one of Marston's most popular teachers.

"It looks like we're going to have another beautiful day." She settled into her seat and brushed dog hairs off her black jumper. "Too nice to be stuck in a classroom."

"Don't let Grimsley hear you say that."

Our principal would react badly to such a comment and, doubtless, issue a reprimand to any teacher heard uttering it.

"It's true," she said. "To top it off, he scheduled a teachers' meeting this afternoon."

"Darn! I forgot about it. I wanted to bake pies today."

"You can still do it."

I could, but I liked to have an early start when baking after school.

"How are you doing with English Lit?" Leonora asked.

This semester I'd lost my American Literature Survey classes and also Journalism, as the Board had elected to cease funding for the school newspaper.

"I take it one day at a time," I said. "Most of the material is new to me."

I had a Master's degree in literature, but I'd never taught it, and had specialized in the Victorian Age. As my new classes were survey courses, we were starting from the very beginning.

"Beowulf and Chaucer instead of Puritan poetry," Leonora said. "I'd call that a good exchange."

"I'll still have some of my major troublemakers from last year, though."

"They're older now."

"Not by much."

I contemplated my new classes and found a huge advantage. Most of the students would be college-bound and committed to earning A's.

Our commute was half country and half freeway. I entered the southbound freeway lane, loath to leave the vibrant colors of the autumn woods behind. Well, it would still be autumn in Oakpoint. My classroom had a breathtaking view of wooded acreage owned by the school.

Mmm. A composition idea for freshman English surfaced. *Describe the view from the window, using concrete and specific words.*

Later, I would ask my ninth graders to use the composition as a setting for a short story.

Much later. First, I needed to determine if they could construct a coherent sentence.

~ * ~

Noise followed me down the hall. Voices loud enough to break the sound barrier. A scream, a snatch of discordant music, lockers banging shut. The ear-splitting ring of the first bell.

Oh, for the incomparable silence of the north woods.

A chatty group of freshmen crowded around the door. I liked to arrive at least fifteen minutes before the first students. Today, I was running late. Leonora, who had stopped at the teachers' lounge for coffee, would be later still.

I unlocked the door and the first arrivals trooped in.

The racket from the hall continued to dog my steps. Maybe my memory was fuzzy, but I remembered my own high school halls being quieter, definitely more orderly. I had carried on conversations with friends, even during class, but no one kept talking when told to be quiet, no one disobeyed an order, and certainly nobody insulted a teacher.

What a rude awakening to teach in a public school! Until I began teaching, I hadn't realized how the norms of olden days had changed.

I turned on the lights, opened my grade book, and waited for the second bell. You would think the freshmen, being in their first class of the day, would be still sleepy, not yet in school mode after the weekend.

You'd be wrong.

As more students streamed in, the noise level rose. Some went straight to their desks. Others roamed around the room, congregating at the windows. When all thirty-four were present, which was practically every day, it was difficult to bridge the gap from chaos to decorum.

Principal Grimsley stopped by the room, peered in, and sent a smile my way. It was the pasted-on smile he wore as if it were an accessory.

The freshmen were loud. You might call them unruly. But the second bell hadn't rung yet. It was free time.

Ah, there it was. The bell and the echo.

The principal moved on.

"All right," I said. "Settle down. Everyone in your seats."

The school day began.

Four

The next day after school, I stopped at the Foxglove Corners Public Library eager to deliver my gift to Miss Eidt.

She always decorated for the seasons. Before long, pumpkins would sprout in the stacks, and the dollhouse, a replica of the actual library, would burst at the seams with tiny decorations. I could imagine how thrilled she would be with the miniature house.

As I walked up to the porch, crimson maple leaves drifted through the air in a mild breeze. Not many, yet. We still had plenty of time to enjoy nature's fall show. The wicker furniture remained in place with Miss Eidt's cat, Blackberry, reclining on a cushion in the best chair. As I approached, she stared at me with her brilliant jewel eyes. Like a stone cat statue, she didn't move in inch.

"Hi, Cat," I murmured as I swept past her and opened the door. The library's fall wreath was unique, decorated with thin wood figures adapted from vintage Halloween greeting cards, and sprinkled with glitter. I wished I could find one just like it.

A leaf blew in with me and settled on the doormat. Miss Eidt sat at her desk surveying her kingdom. She always looked cool and collected, today in a pale lavender dress with a two-strand pearl necklace. The library was blessedly quiet and calm with everyone reading or looking for a book. I felt renewed just stepping through the door.

"Hello, Jennet," she said with her usual warm, welcoming smile. "What brings you here on a school day?"

"I have a present for you from the Apple Fair." I handed her the house which I'd wrapped in orange tissue paper.

"How lovely! I didn't have a chance to attend this year."

"I thought it would be a novel addition to the Gothic Nook."

"Clever pun."

She lifted the house from its nest of tissue and fell silent. Was it my imagination, or did her face lose a layer of its rosy color?

"Oh, my," she said. "This is—different."

I'd never heard a less enthusiastic comment from the recipient of a gift.

"It's for the Gothic Nook," I repeated. "I thought you could set it under one of the Tiffany lamps. It's truly the essence of Gothic."

She touched a gable lightly and withdrew her hand as if the little house had burned her. "You found it at the Apple Fair?"

"At a craft's booth," I said. "It's one of a kind. I thought of you as soon as I saw it. I know you like miniatures. I do, too—"

I trailed off. Why did I feel as if I'd made an embarrassing *faux pas*? Like I had gifted her with a present which she'd previously given me?

She gave the house a small push. It came to rest next to the vase of orange and white carnations at the edge of her desk.

"Thank you," she said. "It's so nice of you to think of me."

"Speaking of the Gothic Nook, do you have anything new?" I asked.

"We found a few paperbacks at an estate sale last week. They weren't in the best shape, but they look good. Debbie patched them up."

Usually, Miss Eidt set aside new finds for me. But, with school starting, I hadn't been in the library for several days. Which shouldn't have made a difference. But—

"What are their titles?" I asked.

She rose. "I can't recall, but I'll go back with you and find them."

"Take the house," I said. "Let's find a good place for it."

"Oh, yes," she said. "The house."

~ * ~

I left the library twenty minutes later with two new/old Gothic paperbacks and an unanswered question that troubled me. Why had Miss Eidt reacted so strangely to the miniature house?

Granted it wasn't edible like the doughnuts or cupcakes I usually brought her from the Hometown Bakery. Still, it was expertly crafted and had a certain charm, one appropriate for the fall season.

Had she hated it at first sight?

Back in the Gothic Nook, she had set it on the nearest table and scanned the shelves quickly as if she knew exactly where the paperbacks were, which was amazing as these books weren't arranged in alphabetical order, and there must be hundreds of them.

"Here they are," she'd said. "*The Master of Blue Mire* and *Masque by Gaslight,* both by Virginia Coffman." She handed them to me. "Happy reading."

As we headed back to the desk, I resolved to look for the house on my next visit to the library. I wondered if it would vanish into a drawer or closet, like unwanted presents the world over.

Darn. I should have kept it.

Outside, I took a deep breath of fresh warm air. The wind had picked up, sending leaves whirling through the air. Blackberry had deserted her post. She had been a feral cat when Miss Eidt decided to adopt her. Occasionally, her wild side surfaced.

I didn't squander a moment worrying about her whereabouts. She had nine lives, after all. I had one, and a homework assignment of my own: compiling background notes for Chaucer's *Canterbury Tales.*

I'd loved Chaucer's stories in my college class, and I should be able to make them palatable to my twenty-first century students in spite of the archaic language. I'd had a fantastic professor, Dr. White. How had he made those characters as real as any we'd meet in our everyday lives and kept us entertained?

Trying to distill his secret, I let the mystery of Miss Eidt and the miniature house from the Apple Fair slip from my mind.

~ * ~

Later, at home, I glanced at the name that appeared on my cell phone.

Whenever Sue Appleton called, it usually concerned collie rescue business and a request. Sometimes, a rescue needed to be picked up at some distance and transported to her horse farm for fostering and eventual rehoming. Now that school had started, I wouldn't be able to take any long trips, and certainly, with seven collies of my own, I couldn't foster any new foundlings.

Sue knew that.

"Hi, Sue," I said. "How are you?"

"I'm well. How's school?"

I could have expounded on that subject for an hour, but all I said was, "So far, so good." So much for small talk.

"What's happening?" I asked.

"Nothing earth-shattering, but I heard something from Ronda Leigh yesterday. I think you'll be interested."

Ronda Leigh was a fairly new member of the Rescue League. She had helped us find the lost collies of Silverhedge.

Sue paused.

"What did you hear?" I asked.

"A friend of Ronda's, Tamryn Lynn, lost her collie some time ago."

"I'm sorry." I waited.

"She's having a difficult time getting over it."

That wasn't surprising. Parting with a beloved pet was like spending time in hell.

Usually, though, the bereft owner came to terms with her loss. Really, what other choice did one have?

"I'm not a grief counselor," I said. "But I can give you the name of one."

"There's something about this that's a bit bizarre," she said. "Something you might be able to help her with."

"What do you want me to do?" I asked.

"For now, just listen. Tamryn had her dog cremated, but she didn't find it comforting to keep the ashes where she could see them, like in a little shrine with the dog's picture. The ashes were adding to her grief."

I could understand that. One's source of comfort could well be another's torment. What I couldn't understand was why Sue thought I could help Tamryn. She had to supply more details.

"Tamryn decided to spread the ashes in her yard under the tree where the dog used to lie. She thought that would help."

"Did it?"

"In a way, but here's the problem. Now, Tamryn thinks that, somehow, she brought her dog back to life. She swears she's seen her under the tree, and lying in front of the gate, looking at the sidewalk. She wishes she could gather the ashes again and put them back in the urn."

Good heavens and shades of Stephen King. Collecting ashes, once sprinkled on the ground, was impossible. As was Sue's latest request.

I asked again, "What do you want me to do?"

"Convince her this isn't happening," she said.

Five

"I don't know what I can do for Ronda's friend," I said. "If she truly believes she brought her dead dog back to life...Well, what can I say?"

"Ronda thinks Tamryn just *wants* to believe it."

"Then she should see a psychologist or a grief counselor."

"Didn't you once see a collie that wasn't there?" Sue asked.

"A ghost dog. Yes. That was different."

Misty, my psychic collie, had detected a canine spirit, Macduff, who had lived in my house long before I'd moved to Foxglove Corners. He was trying to find the family that had abandoned him.

"How is it different?" she asked.

I had to think about that. How to explain it?

"Macduff was there," I said. "Lucy saw him, too. I didn't create him."

"This is Foxglove Corners where strange things have been known to happen," Sue reminded me.

"I can't argue with that."

"Will you at least meet Tamryn?"

"I suppose I can. But what does Ronda think I can do for her?"

"You'll have to ask her," Sue said. "My understanding is that

Tamryn wants to understand what's happening. You're the expert on strange occurrences in Foxglove Corners."

Someday, I hoped to live down my reputation. Or live up to it.

I agreed to meet Ronda and Tamryn at Sue's house when both could arrange it and ended the call.

This was exactly what I needed in my life. A little Halloween spookiness.

~ * ~

Every now and then, Brent Fowler, Foxglove Corners' red-haired fox hunter, entrepreneur, and man about town, descended on us unannounced at the dinner hour. He brought candy or flowers for the house and treats for the collies in a gift bag from Pluto's Gourmet Pet Shop. Fortunately, tonight I had cooked enough to feed all of us—a pot roast with potatoes and carrots.

We hadn't seen Brent for a while, not since school started. I assumed he had thrown himself into another undertaking.

Crane relocated the candy to safety on the mantel while Brent dispensed a venison tart each to the impatiently waiting collies. He handed me the empty bag and settled himself in the rocker.

"Where've you been keeping yourself, Fowler?" Crane asked.

"At the barn, mostly. Hanging out with the Hunt. This fall we've had great hunting weather."

He patted his knee. Misty leaped into his lap, and Sky settled down at his feet, licking crumbs from her muzzle. They adored him. Candy led the rest of the pack into the kitchen to monitor the roast in my absence.

Brent didn't sound particularly enthusiastic. I was ambivalent about his association with the Foxglove Corners Hunt Club and his special friend, Alethea Venn. Brent was the most compassionate and humane person I knew, and he had the funds to reinforce his principles. As for the Hunt Club, I considered it an archaic institution more suitable for England or Virginia.

As for Alethea, I simply didn't like her.

"Is anything wrong?" I asked.

"Everything's going my way for once," he said. "We're taking care of ten geriatric collies at the Loosestrife Lane house. Lila and Letty

Woodville are happy with their new position as caregivers. The ghosts are quiet."

He glanced out the bay window where an array of glorious fall colors rivaled any crimson and gold landscape in a frame. "I'm bored. I need a new project."

"A new mission," I murmured.

"Yes."

"There are plenty of causes in Foxglove Corners that need help," Crane pointed out.

"Name one."

"Collecting clothes and toys for orphans. We do that at the station year-around. People are generous at Christmastime, but there are eleven other months in the year."

Brent said. "I could do that."

But I knew Brent preferred to buy toys and clothes new and deliver them to needy children in Foxglove Corners at Christmas.

"You like to work with animals," I said. "How about horses? It seems I'm always reading about neglected horses. Herds of them out West are in danger of being slaughtered. They need sanctuaries. That requires money."

"The idea to move geriatric collies into a house of their own just came to me," he said. "I knew it was right, and I was excited about it. Helping wild horses in the West is too remote."

I didn't agree with him but didn't argue. He had to be committed to a project to throw his heart into it.

"You'll find your next cause," I assured him. "Let it come to you naturally. Don't force it."

I was tempted to tell him that he could help me solve the mystery of Tamryn's resurrected collie, but her problem wasn't mine to share. Likewise, Miss Eidt's aversion to the little house from the Apple Fair was too personal and, at the moment, nebulous.

"I could take a trip," he said. "But Foxglove Corners is so beautiful this time of year."

I nodded. "Wait until the leaves are gone, and we all want to escape from cold and snow. Then find a place where it's summer again."

"That's a plan," he said.

"In the meantime, something may come up."

A worthy project Brent could sink his teeth into. I was unused to seeing him flounder.

Happily, he changed the subject. "Something smells good."

"It must be the pot roast," I said. "Or maybe the apple pie."

"Do you have enough for three?" he asked.

"Of course. And leftovers for seven collies."

"When do we eat?"

"Soon. Let me check on the roast."

I had to wade through collies to reach the stove. Candy stood at my side, aiming her long nose toward the roaster, in danger of getting burned. I ordered her to move and stuck a fork into the meat. Done and savory. The liquids were bubbling, and the pie on the counterwas still warm. The dishes and candlesticks were on the table. I'd just add another placesetting.

"Ten minutes," I called into the living room, and Misty and Sky joined the rest ofthe pack in the kitchen.

~ * ~

Leonora had taken a sick day to nurse a cold. The substitute teacher had let her classes run wild—literally. At the end of the day, exhausted by the mayhem in the classroom next to mine, I'd stopped at Clovers for take-out dinners. Yesterday's roast had disappeared into sandwiches and leftovers for the collies.

Annica's bright smile was missing. Her dress was beige, her earrings faux acorns, and she wore an open collared cream cardigan, none of which did justice to her natural glow and red-gold hair.

It was Pumpkin Week at Clovers, judging by the pies and tarts in the dessert carousel. By rights, she should be wearing orange.

I seated myself in my favorite booth with the best view of the woods across from Crispian Road.

Annica set a tall glass of water and a menu in front of me. "How did Miss Eidt like her miniature house?"

"I'm not sure, but I don't think she did."

"Why not?"

"She didn't say."

"Maybe she's more the pastel country cottage type."

I took a sip of water and ordered two meatloaf dinners and a lime cooler, most likely the last one of the season. "I tried."

Annica whispered to Marcy, her fellow waitress who always covered for her when I visited Clovers and returned presently with our drinks.

"How's our little pie thief?" she asked.

"Sue thinks she has a good home for her, but it isn't official yet."

"That's good. What else is new?"

"Nothing, except my classes."

Before I could expound on the woes of a high school English teacher, Annica said, "I miss all the excitement we had last summer. And before, when we discovered the ghost town. Nothing ever happens anymore. It's just reading long boring novels for school and slinging hash."

"When did you ever sling hash?" I asked. "I didn't know it was on the menu."

"It's just an expression."

"You could drive out to the wildflower field and look for ghosts," I said.

I meant the field on Huron Court where Annica had seen a spirit gathering flowers for a heavenly bouquet.

"I did that. Most of the flowers are dying."

"That happens in October."

"Some are still in good shape. I saw a few daisies with red petals. They're pretty tall, like sunflowers. But the field won't be interesting until next summer."

Annica sounded a little like Brent, lost without a special dream to pursue.

My lime cooler was rapidly vanishing, like the lazy summer days. I preferred to look to the future rather than wallow in the past.

"You sound depressed," I said. "Is everything all right?"

"I guess so." She sighed. "It's just that all the really exciting things have already happened. What if there's nothing left?"

Six

A line of linden trees shaded the north side of Sue Appleton's corral. The sun, which had given us one of those rare summer-warm days, hung low in a cloudless blue sky. It transformed the yellow leaves to pure, glittering gold.

Behind the fence, horses grazed, and collies frolicked around the ranch house, turning my thoughts to art. To life, even though our conversation leaned heavily on death and loss. Only Velvet preferred to lie on the porch with us and beg for the sugar cookies Sue had served with lemonade.

Or perhaps the attraction was Tamryn Lynn, who had scarcely taken her hand from Velvet's head. Tamryn was younger than the Mother Goose character I'd imagined, with dark blonde hair cut in a pageboy style. She wore blue jeans and a shirt that boldly proclaimed, *Me Too*. The frames of her glasses glittered with tiny pink stones. I had no idea where the Mother Goose image had come from. Ronda Leigh hadn't been able to join her, having come down with a cold.

"I miss my Cara so much," Tamryn said. "My house is empty now. So is my heart."

"Is it too early for you to think of adopting another collie?" Sue asked.

"Oh, yes. First I have to know if Cara is still with me."

Ah! We'd arrived at the heart of the matter. What exactly had she meant by saying 'with me'?

I took refuge in my sugar cookie while Sue refilled our glasses.

"I mention this because we have some lovely collies ready for adoption," Sue said, setting the empty pitcher on a side table. "They lost their homes through no fault of their own."

She said this, although she didn't know the backgrounds of most of the collies who came into rescue. Velvet, for example. For all anyone knew, she had fallen from the sky to earth to wander through the Apple Fair.

Finally I said, "You've buried Cara in your heart, so of course she's still with you."

"It's natural for you to feel guilty, but you were thinking of her," Sue added. "My uncle died recently after a debilitating illness. We can't legally or morally help people cross over to the other side. Well, not in Michigan. In that sense, our dogs and cats are luckier."

"And remember," I added, "Pope Francis said we'd see our animals again." Of all his pronouncements, that was the one I held close to my heart.

"I believe that," Tamryn said. "So why doesn't it help? When I lost Cara, I made a little shrine for her with my favorite pictures, her collar, and her ashes in the box they came in. But it didn't comfort me. Just the opposite. Every time I passed it, I felt the grief of losing her all over again. Finally, I took the shrine apart and scattered her ashes around the tree she used to lie under."

"That's one way to cope," I said.

"It backfired." She turned to me. "Did Sue tell you what happened?"

"She said something about it."

"The very next day, I saw Cara lying under the tree. It was late, but there was plenty of moonlight. Cara was a tri, mostly black, and it isn't easy to see her in the dark; but she was there. I'll swear to it."

"Do you think you saw a ghost?" I asked.

"No. I saw her. There was nothing ghostly about her."

"Did you call her?"

"I was in shock that first time. I thought I was imagining it. Then I looked again, and she was gone."

"Shadows," Sue murmured. "At the end of the day, the ranch fills up with them. I've seen some odd shapes myself when I'm out with the dogs before bedtime."

"It wasn't a shadow."

"You referred to a first time," I said. "You must have seen her again, then."

"I did, two more times, around the same time in the same place. I called her name, but she just stared at me. After a few minutes, she faded into the background. The last time it happened, I walked over to the tree and found this."

She drew a small tag out of her pocket. It was a shiny bone-shaped sliver of tin with Cara's name engraved on it.

Now this was weird.

"Was it separated from Cara before she was—cremated?" I stumbled over that last word.

"It wasn't in the box with her ashes. The last time I saw the tag, Cara was wearing it."

I shied away from eerie mysteries with no apparent solution. Consequently, I pushed this one out of the equation. I decided to voice what I was thinking, and hope Tamryn wouldn't be offended. She shouldn't be. She'd raised the possibility with Sue.

"Do you think scattering the ashes somehow caused Cara to appear?" I was going to add 'to re-assemble herself' but didn't. It would make Cara sound like a puzzle. Or a clone.

"I don't know how else to explain it," Tamryn said.

I did. As Sue had pointed out, Tamryn felt guilty for having Cara euthanized, which was natural. Mix grief with guilt, and the effect of living uneasily with a beloved pet's ashes, and you have a potent elixir.

"You realize that simply isn't possible, outside of *Pet Sematary*, that is."

"Then tell me what has been visiting my backyard."

I couldn't do that. I glanced at Sue, hoping she could steer the conversation in a different direction. She took the hint.

"As you know, we rescue lost or abandoned collies," she said. "Jennet came across Velvet days ago at the Apple Fair. My point is, there are a lot of strays running free in the country. Sometimes their owners deliberately drop them off, thinking a farmer will take them in. That rarely happens."

"That's where we come in," I added.

"I didn't see a stray." A note of irritation crept into Tamryn's tone. "I would know my Cara anywhere. I've had her since she was six weeks old. She was a beautiful tri with a broken collar, more white on her right side than left. And she had a blaze."

"How could you see these details in the dark?" Sue asked.

Sidestepping the question, Tamryn said, "I know my dog."

I still didn't understand my role into Tamryn's tone. How was I supposed to help her other than recommend a grief counselor?

Ask her.

"How can I help you, Tamryn?"

"I heard you were an expert on supernatural phenomena."

Again, I glanced at Sue. She shrugged.

"From who? I mean, whom?"

"Someone at the library."

"From Miss Eidt?"

"No, from a lady I met there. Her name is Edwina."

Edwina Endicott, Foxglove Corner's self-proclaimed ghost catcher. I considered Edwina fifty percent authentic and fifty percent delusional.

"Maybe Ms. Endicott can help you. But I'm confused. You said you didn't think this thing—er Cara—was a ghost."

"I don't, but if I could eliminate the possibility..." She trailed off and hooked her fingers under Velvet's collar. Velvet tried to back up, then sat, willing to endure additional petting.

"Then?" I asked.

"Then I'd know I brought Cara back to life."

Sue's sigh was audible. She was silent. I had already told Tamryn that what she believed was impossible. What more could I say? I had no idea how to prove that an odd phenomenon wasn't a spirit.

Tell her then. Say that.

"I'll try to help you," I said, "but you have to be more specific. What do you want me to do?"

"If you could come to my house around seven o'clock some evening and see if Cara is there."

I frowned. "How do you know she'll choose that time to appear?"

Faint color touched her face. "I wasn't strictly speaking honest with you when I said I'd seen Cara three times, Jennet. She appears in the yard every night."

~ * ~

"Well," Sue said as we watched Tamryn drive slowly down to Squill Lane. "What do you think?"

"That Tamryn is seriously in need of help. Maybe she was always this way. Losing Cara pushed her over the edge."

"How do you explain the name tag?"

"All we know about that is what Tamryn told us."

"I'm not at my best with people who have such a loose grip on reality," I said. Which was putting it mildly.

"I wanted to ask her if she'd want Cara back under the circumstances," Sue said. "I keep thinking about *Pet Sematary*, and that awful little story, *The Monkey's Paw*. If Cara had really died and been brought back to life, she'd be different."

"And I almost asked her how she thought this transformation worked. If the ashes had reassembled themselves into a collie."

"I found the card of a grief counselor," Sue said. "I didn't think tonight was the right time to mention it, though."

"Hold onto it," I said. "Now that we know the situation, we can't leave Tamryn to deal with this on her own."

"What are you going to do?" Sue asked.

"What she asked. I'll pay her a visit and check it out."

She had mentioned Friday at seven o'clock. I could already see Crane's face when I told him where I was going and why.

"What if you don't see the dog? Which you won't, of course."

I shook my head. "I'll take it from there."

Seven

Several pies, muffins, and a coffee cake later, I discovered that I was out of apples. The Fair in Maple Creek was a distant memory. Last night a thunderstorm and high winds had brought down an alarming number of leaves. These precious, golden days of fall were short-lived. Before I knew it, the trees would be bare, and the cider mills shuttered for the season.

Make haste, Mother Nature whispered. *Another month and Foxglove Corners will sleep under a blanket of snow.*

For some reason, I was thinking about caramel apples. When those images faded, I replaced them with doughnuts and jugs of cider.

As it was Saturday, I decided on a quick trip to the Brightwater Cider Mill. And as I knew Annica had the day off and was caught up—sort of—on her reading, I invited her to ride along with me.

"I'm glad we're doing this," she said. "I am *so* ready for a new adventure."

"I wouldn't call a drive to the cider mill an adventure."

It felt like one, though. To go somewhere—anywhere—new on a bright October morning and leave my 'to do' list behind was invigorating. Annica may have been caught up on her reading, but I had to keep one step ahead of my English Lit classes.

"Do you know the way?" she asked.

"Vaguely. I've only been there once. Keep the map handy."

"This reminds me of the time we found Ashton."

She referred to the ghost town we first thought was named Forever.

"Once you venture beyond familiar boundaries, who knows what you'll find?" I said. "That sounds like a lead-in to a *Twilight Zone* episode."

"It does, but all I'm hoping to find are apples." I glanced at her. "Are you over your malaise?"

"I have to be. One of my classes is a seminar with only seven members. We were hand-picked by our Victorian Novels professor. Every Friday we have to come up with something brilliant to say about the week's book."

I smiled. "Oh, the pressure."

"I'm reading *Doctor Thorne*. Are you familiar with it?"

"It doesn't ring a bell."

"I hoped you could give me a sentence or two."

"Sorry."

We were traveling on a road with deep forest on either side, state land, I believed. When we reached its end, if that ever happened, I'd have to consult the map. Meanwhile, I enjoyed the passing color show. Streaks of crimson and gold wove their way through an endless stretch of dark green conifers and blue spruce.

The scenery was breathtaking, but downed leaves made the narrow road slippery in places. I couldn't afford to let my mind wander.

"I'm going to pull over and have a look at the map," I said. "And plot a course?"

"Yes. We don't want to find we're heading in the wrong direction."

The chance of getting lost was slight, but the quick breakfast we'd had at Clovers hadn't made a dent in the appetite that goes along with a mini road trip. I was hungry and could hardly wait to feast on apples and the assorted treats any cider mill worth its salt offered.

Our new course took us away from forest and plunged us into farm country with spent fields ready for their long winter nap. Horses grazed placidly behind their fences, and hulking barns rose against a background of deep blue sky. Houses were few and far between, and, for the most part, built far from the road.

Except for one.

Dark and brooding with multiple gables, the house stood alone on its many-acred parcel, looking as if it had been in that location since the dawn of time. It appeared to hide behind a stand of crimson maple trees that gave it much needed color and added to the initial impression of secrecy.

I brought the Focus to a rolling stop, admiring the architecture, and counting the seven gables. An entrancing study in dark brown with gray stonework and charcoal siding, it reminded me of the house in Nathaniel Hawthorne's novel.

A sense of *déjà vu* dropped down on me. I had seen this house somewhere before. In a nightmare?

"How spooky," Annica said. "I wonder if it's haunted."

"It looks like it could be."

I didn't see any signs of habitation and the house had no neighbors. No car parked in the broken concrete driveway, no curtains hung in the windows, no smoke spiraled up from the chimney. Fallen leaves covered the lawn. They hid the pathway to the porch, if indeed one existed.

In the back, a scarecrow was placed so that it appeared to peer around the house's west side, as if its sole mission was to discourage visitors.

Where had I seen this house before? Or one like it?

"It doesn't need a single Halloween decoration," Annica said. "It isn't particularly appealing, but there's something about it—"

Suddenly, I knew why it was so familiar.

"It's a life-sized version of the house I bought for Miss Eidt," I said. "I'd have to see it again, but I'll swear this is a mirror image."

"You're right."

"Let's see if anyone is at home."

"And say what? We were just in the neighborhood?"

"Put the map in the glove apartment. We'll say we got lost on our way to the Brightwater Cider Mill."

We crunched our way up to the wide porch where more leaves had congregated, forming high mounds in the corners.

I looked through the front window and saw a large empty room. The people had moved out. How long ago? Most likely before the leaves started falling. I didn't see a 'For Sale' sign, which only meant the house wasn't listed with a realtor yet or wouldn't be.

"No sense knocking," Annica said.

I agreed. "I'd like to come back with the little house I gave Miss Eidt to compare the two."

"How are you going to get it away from her?"

"Probably tell her the truth."

Judging from her lukewarm reception of my gift, convincing her to return it wouldn't be difficult.

I glanced back at the downward slope of land that rolled away into the distance. All I could see was a spent field that seemed to go on forever and the guardian scarecrow.

"Let's check out the scarecrow," I said, walking around to the back. Then, "For the love of...Look!"

Not one but several scarecrows stood behind the house, spaced at intervals but so close together, I thought of them as a macabre gathering. They put me in mind of sentinels, protecting the house from...What? The field? In any event, their many different outfits splashed the monochromatic vista with vibrant color. I counted twelve of them.

"Wow!" Annica said. "Correct me if I'm wrong, but don't farmers usually settle for one scarecrow per field?"

"I never gave the matter any thought, but offhand I'd say you're right."

She brought out her phone and aimed it at the group. "I have to take a picture of this."

"It's enough to scare a crow to death," I said.

She took her picture, then two more, after which she walked from one scarecrow to another.

"They're all wearing different outfits," she said.

"And none of them looks like typical scarecrow wear. Isn't the idea to dress a scarecrow in old, outlandish clothes?"

"I suppose so."

"Then these are unique."

I once encountered a woman whose hobby was dressing scarecrows to sell as autumn decorations for house and yard. The one she'd given us currently lived in the basement. As I recalled, it wore jeans with large holes cut into the material, a tattered shirt, and an oversized hat trimmed with green roses.

I surveyed the congregation of scarecrows, aware of a chill creeping into my veins. The unexpected, bizarre sight spoke of something fearful, a slumbering evil.

Fearful? Evil? They were simply creations of straw and clothing. Not creatures.

"They are really, really weird," I said.

Pausing before a scarecrow wearing a patchwork cotton skirt, a red crew neck sweater and a garish curly blonde wig, I said, "This one has a nametag," I said. "She's Maisie."

Annica snapped another picture. "They all do. I'm looking at Clarabella."

Behind Clarabella stood Harvey, dressed in a purple jumpsuit with an ankle-length cape. A Dracula mask hid the lump of whitish canvas that served as his face.

My eyes moved from one to another. I examined them, looking for name tags. "And here's Mabel. And Lancelot. This one is Dolly. There's a whole family back here. Or a group of friends."

Or a congregation of fiends.

Eight

After the encounter with the scarecrows, our visit to the cider mill was anti-climactic. We loaded the cart with apples, cider and doughnuts, our conversation stalled on the subject of scarecrows.

"It looks like we have a new mystery," Annica said.

"One that may not be easy to solve with no one living in the house."

I took another doughnut from the Brightwater Bakery bag. At this rate, they wouldn't make it home.

"That never stopped us before," Annica pointed out.

"What puzzles me is that peculiar placement. I assume all the land belongs to whoever owns the house. Why wouldn't the people spread the scarecrows out in the fields?"

An idea I'd had on first seeing them tugged at me. "It looks like their purpose is to protect the house."

"From what? Birds? Like in that Alfred Hitchcock movie?"

I smiled. "From crows, of course." I didn't care for that nightmare-inducing movie. Any creature that appeared in multiples gave me pause.

Even the thought of the Hitchcock chiller created unwelcome images in mind. A cloud of black birds on the rampage, flying through the field, lighting on this shoulder or that head, impossible to escape. Nightmare stuff.

"Right now, I'm more interested in Miss Eidt's connection to the house, if there is one," I said.

I wouldn't have thought that our gentle librarian in her pastel suits and pearl necklaces harbored a secret. Or, if she did, that she would be willing to reveal it, being an extremely private person.

Annica glanced at the counters with their wondrous apple offerings, shopping list in hand. "Let's buy caramel apples for the road."

"I'll stick with doughnuts. In fact, I'd better buy another dozen."

For the road.

On our way home, we would drive past the house of scarecrows again. Our new mystery wasn't an hour old, but in my mind, I was already moving ahead to Step Two: coming back to the strange house of scarecrows with the miniature duplicate that had quite likely inspired it.

~ * ~

The next day after dropping Leonora off at home, I drove to the library. Steeped in late afternoon sunshine and silence, the old white Victorian seemed to be sinking in a sea of leaves. Neither Miss Eidt nor Debbie had raked them, but someone had scattered pumpkins and gourds along the façade, and on the porch.

Only the walkway remained relatively clear. Blackberry was in her usual place in the rocker as motionless as a stone statue, fixing her jewel-eyed stare on all comers. A bright orange ribbon circled her neck, turning her into a living Halloween decoration.

As I didn't see Miss Eidt at her desk, I wandered back to the Gothic Nook. The miniature replica of the Scarecrow House was nowhere in sight. Under the Tiffany style lamp where I'd imagined she would place it, an imitation pumpkin with a sinister sneer filled the corner with faux candlelight.

Never passing up the chance to look for the quintessential Gothic novel, I scanned the shelves and almost at once found a true treasure, a pristine copy of *Haldane Station* by Florence Engel Randall in mint condition. I'd read it before but didn't own a copy, and this one could have come directly from a bookstore.

By the time I brought the book up to the checkout desk, Miss Eidt was back at her station, unpacking small boxes that contained the miniature furnishings of the library dollhouse which stood on a table in the paperback carousel's usual spot. The carousel had been moved to the left.

She set a tiny dining room table and four matching chairs in a group with similar furniture. "I didn't see you come in, Jennet."

"I found this book in the Gothic Nook," I said. "It's an amazing story. I wish the author were still living and writing."

She stared at it as if it were another object. "*Haldane Station*. I don't recall seeing this. Debbie must have handled it."

As she stamped the book, I said, "I've come to ask a favor. That little house I brought you from the Apple Fair...Could I borrow I back? Just for a few days?"

She frowned. "Certainly. May I ask why?"

"I came across a house with a remarkable resemblance to it. I'd like to compare them."

"I see."

"You still have it, don't you?"

She hesitated. "Yes, of course. It's in my office."

In her office? On the table where she could see it whenever she took a break with a cup of coffee? Or shut away in a cupboard?

"Where did you see this house?" she asked.

I opened my mouth to answer and realized I didn't know. "I don't remember, but it was on the way to the Brightwater Cider Mill. About fifteen minutes from it."

"Could it be Mill Road?"

"That's it. Oh, one more detail, the most important," I added. "There were a dozen scarecrows behind it."

"So many? How odd."

"We thought so."

"Did you ask the homeowner about them?"

"The house was vacant," I said. "I assume it was for sale, but there was no sign."

I was going to tell her about the way the scarecrows had been dressed and given names, but her lack of interest discouraged me.

"A lot of those old farm houses look alike," she said.

That was true. "But this one had unique architectural features. That's why I want to compare them."

Something was different about Miss Eidt today. Usually she was curious about matters I brought to her attention, eager to know more and to help, if possible. At present, she seemed more than preoccupied. Almost anxious. Afraid? But that was ridiculous. How could a small hand-carved object be a source of fear?

"Just a minute," she said. "I'll get it."

Left alone at the desk, I glanced at the dollhouse waiting patiently for its furnishings, the tiny doll people who inhabited it, and the fall/Halloween trimmings. It served as a reminder that the library was the home where Miss Eidt had grown up. She always made sure that anyone who admired the dollhouse knew its history, and that she had played with it as a child.

She set the Apple Fair house on the desk. In the brief awkward silence that followed, I said, "The library looks nice and festive."

"We're getting there. I'm going to have a Halloween party. This year I'm encouraging people to dress as characters from their favorite book."

Halloween parties in Foxglove Corners have a reputation for luring villains out of the woodwork. At a party in my own house, before Crane and I were married, I had matched wits with a clever killer, and last year, I'd been abducted from this very library by a sinister pirate.

Bring on the ghouls!

"I could dress as a Gothic heroine," I said. "I'd find a pretty nineteenth century costume and carry a candlestick."

"No one would know who you were," she pointed out. "I'm going to reprise my role as the Queen of Hearts. There'll be a special prize for the best costume."

"What is it?" I asked.

"Ah, that's my secret."

"I still have my pointed witch's hat," I said, "and plenty of black dresses and jewelry." Even a bottle of black fingernail polish.

"Whatever you choose will be fine."

Now she sounded like her old self; the gentle, serene lady who ruled the library with an iron hand. I thought fleetingly about asking her what troubled her about the house from the Apple Fair. In this mood, she would be likely to tell me. In the end, though, I decided to wait for her to confide in me, which she would if she wanted me to know. If not, then it would remain a mystery.

I picked up *Haldane Station* and the miniature house. "I'll bring it back to you in a day or two with a picture of the original."

"No hurry," she said and reached for another box.

Was I the only one who thought the little house was important?

Nine

I'd just settled down with a cup of tea, a muffin, and *Haldane Station* when my cell phone's rippling notes summoned me back to the real world.

It was Tamryn. Again. She'd just called yesterday.

"I'm sorry to have to postpone our visit again, Jennet, but something came up," she said. "Could you come another time? I'll let you know when I'm free."

"I suppose so." I set the cup on the coffee table. "What day did you have in mind?"

"Let me call you."

What could I do but agree? Still, as I set my phone down, I wondered about her sincerity.

I'd thought the apparent resurrection of her lost collie was her primary concern, the reason she had practically begged me to investigate the phenomenon. Why, then, did she allow something to come up? This was the second time she had cancelled our appointment.

"You're dealing with a deluded woman, Jennet," Crane said when I told him about the change in plans. "She needs to see a grief counselor."

"She insists she brought her dog back to life by scattering its ashes in her backyard. Therefore, there's no need for grief."

"That's crazy."

"That's the problem."

In Tamryn's mind, if she knew she would see Cara under the lilac tree every day, she could avoid acknowledging the loss. When I failed to see this imagined dog, however, eventually she'd have to say goodbye to her delusion. Which explained the two postponements. Maybe.

What I didn't understand was why she was willing to take the risk of my not seeing Cara. Why not just enjoy the make-believe while it lasted?

Well, Tamryn's mental state of mind wasn't my concern.

"I've been thinking," I said, "if we were to lose a collie, heaven forbid, I'd like her buried on our own property."

I couldn't bear to think of one of our beautiful, lively collies reduced to a pile of ashes in a metal container. Or like crimson leaves disintegrating when they reached the ground, becoming one with the earth. No. To me, cremation was a fearful word.

Crane's expression was grave. "We'll cross that bridge when we come to it."

"I know."

Misty had sidled up to me. She knew I had an apple muffin—her new favorite—wrapped in a napkin on my lap. She nudged my hand and sat back, head tilted. Who claimed that dogs can't talk? I didn't have to eat the muffin this minute and soon she'd be distracted. Usually I'd share, but this was the last one. All right, I was selfish.

"When I die, I don't want to be cremated," I said. "I'm afraid of fire."

Like many people, Crane and I had avoided talking about the inevitable, that one day death would do us part.

I'm going to live forever, I thought. *Well, not really, but I refuse to worry about it today.*

Today is for living.

"On the other hand, I don't want to be buried in the ground," I said. "I've read too many Edgar Allen Poe tales about people being buried alive."

"Not in this century," Crane pointed out. "Besides, you're talking about story characters."

"But it's happened in real life. I've read about cases—"

"Let's change the subject," he said. "Are you going back to the cider mill soon? We're almost out of doughnuts."

"I can go tomorrow now that Tamryn doesn't want me to check out her impossible re-created collie."

Yes, tomorrow after school while the good weather held. Images of sparkling apple cider and warm, crisp doughnuts chased away thoughts of death. And on the way to the cider mill, I would drive by the Scarecrow House and compare it to the miniature duplicate. While there, I'd take a picture to show Miss Eidt.

I took another sip of tea and returned to *Haldane Station*, to the rather confusing opening scene that paved the way for the delicious time twist to come.

As for Tamryn, if she postponed my visit a third time, I'd be unavailable for further consultation.

~ * ~

The next day after school, Leonora and I took a detour to the cider mill. The weather was perfect with a deep blue sky, a light wind, and ever-changing autumn color in every direction.

"I'm going to buy some apples and bake pies tonight," Leonora said. "Jake loves my pies."

She had moved the small replica of the Scarecrow House from the passenger seat but held on to it, running her fingers along every inch of it, every dollop of gingerbread trim, and every minute decoration.

"Whoever carved this little house was a true artist," she said.

"It's one of a kind, or so I was told."

"For me, the appeal of a tiny house like this is imagining the life going on behind the windows. That's why I loved to play with my dollhouse. I still have it," she added.

"You don't still play with it, I hope."

"It's stored in the attic. Maybe if Jake and I have children—" She trailed off.

Setting aside the idea of saving childhood toys, which I hadn't done, I said, "What kind of life?"

"You know. Who lives there? What they're doing. Is the mother in the kitchen making dinner? What about the kids? Are they happy?"

Her rambling reminded me of the Scarecrow House, the big one. At present it was vacant, but who had lived there once? Someone whose hobby was crafting scarecrows?

I wished I knew everything about them, while realizing that I was unlikely to satisfy my curiosity any time soon.

A few minutes after I turned on the road that would take us to the cider mill, the light drained out of the blue sky. The winds picked up, shaking leaves down to the ground. They stuck to the windows with splatters of rain. I turned on the windshield wipers.

"What happened?" Leonora said.

"A little change in the weather. Fall is unpredictable."

"But a minute ago the sun was shining."

"Don't worry," I said. "I have an umbrella in the trunk."

We were going to need it. In seconds, the splatters turned into heavy rain pelting the car.

But I *did* worry...about the pictures I wanted to take. How could I capture the scarecrows' images in this downpour?

~ * ~

By the time we'd completed our raid on the cider mill, the brief storm had moved on.

The sun returned, bringing enough light to guarantee good pictures. Except for the fresh-washed earth, the rain might never have happened.

At the Scarecrow House, I parked the Focus in the driveway and took my cell phone out of my handbag.

"Do you want to come with me?" I asked.

"Definitely. I have to see these marvelous scarecrows."

We walked around to the back of the house, trying to dodge raindrops that dripped down from the sodden leaves. The earth had a wondrous fresh smell and the scarecrows looked as if they'd had a spin in a washing machine.

"Amazing," Leonora said. "Their maker gave them names. How cute."

"Each one is different," I said. "Differently dressed, that is. I suppose their bodies came from the same mold."

"Yeah, straw." She touched Maisie's bright orange blouse. "It feels like silk."

"This is getting weird," I said. "Who puts a silk blouse on a scarecrow?"

I went from one scarecrow to another, taking pictures for Miss Eidt. I hoped she knew something about the house and that, when I showed them to her, she would break down and tell me what she knew.

Why did I have the feeling I was being watched? That the watchers disapproved of my presence, and the pictures I was taking? That I was in danger?

Don't be silly, I told myself. *You can dress a scarecrow in fancy attire, but you can't give it eyes.*

On the fringe of the ghostly gathering stood a scarecrow I didn't remember seeing.

Partially hidden from my view by the scarecrow in front of her, she wore a long white dress with a sequined bodice. Bat wing sleeves and a short white veil flapped in the wind.

The scarecrow bride.

Her name was Adelaide.

I hadn't seen her before. I was certain of it.

Quelling a sense of rising panic, I counted. Four...Seven...Nine... There had been an even dozen scarecrows before.

Now there were thirteen.

Ten

The feeling of being watched intensified. I could almost hear a voice in the wind: *Get out! You don't belong here.*

Something was spying on us, and it wasn't a dozen sightless scarecrows. I stepped back from the Scarecrow Bride and surveyed all the windows on the back of the house. No curtains, no sign of watchers. Nothing was moving. Only a hint of malice in the air so thick I could practically touch it.

Leonora pulled back the veil from the scarecrow's straw head. "This is criminal, Jennet."

"What is?"

"Leaving this beautiful veil outside for the weather to ravage."

I looked more closely at the headpiece, seeing details I'd missed, like lace inserts and sparkling sequins on material as light as air. The veil must have been expensive, perhaps custom made, along with the dress.

Once again, not typical scarecrow wear.

"We assumed the house was vacant and probably it is, but someone came back recently and added this thirteenth scarecrow. I'm wondering who and why. The homeowners? The realtor? Some local prankster?"

"Lucy believes thirteen is an unlucky number," Leonora reminded me.

That was true. She had once asked Brent to add another guest to his dinner party, afraid to jinx *Devilwish,* the movie based on her book, by leaving the number of diners at thirteen.

"Unlucky for scavengers," I murmured. "It must be working. I don't see any birds at all."

Leonora glanced at the darkening sky. "I feel like taking the bride's veil home with me."

"You can't do that. It'd be stealing."

"I guess. But not in this case. I'm going to do it."

She removed the veil gently, leaving the top of the straw head bare to the elements.

We were already trespassing on private property. Now that I knew the miniature house from the Apple Fair was the mirror image of the Scarecrow House, down to the last unique architectural detail, we had no reason to linger on the property. We'd better leave.

Suddenly, suspecting that we were being observed, our conversation carried through the walls, I looked once again at the windows.

Go away! Get out of here!

The Scarecrow House was capable of a strange form of communication. Or my imagination was running amok.

"We'd better go before it starts raining again," I said. "Or before someone comes along with a shotgun."

Leonora was already walking toward the car, the veil fluttering in her hand. For a moment, it reminded me of a captive white bird, trying desperately to escape.

"If that happens, I'll die." She spoke lightly, but her choice of words sounded a faint alarm.

"Don't say that."

"What?"

"Die. To die in a deserted cornfield isn't part of my day's plan."

"Don't overreact," she said. "It's just an expression."

~ * ~

Safe at home, I listened to my collies' greeting. They were loud enough to wake the proverbial dead, and I could see faces in the window. Halley and Candy. They'd have to wait a few more minutes.

I lifted a bushel of apples out of the trunk and carried it across the lane to the magnificent yellow Victorian with its wide wraparound porch. The wreath on Camille's door was similar to the one that decorated the library with woodcut Halloween decorations inspired by vintage greeting cards. The candy corn looked real enough to eat, and the witch smiled with wicked glee as she brandished an oversized spoon.

Ironically, Camille had a large spoon in her hand when she opened the door. Her smile, however, was warm and inviting. Holly and Twister dashed out to the porch to dance around my legs and sniff at the bushel.

"I brought you some apples from the cider mill," I said.

"How lovely! I'll turn them into pies and tarts."

"That's what I'm going to do with mine."

"Come in and have a cup of tea with me. I'm due for a break."

The yellow Victorian always smelled of something sweet…today of pumpkins and spice. I sat and helped myself to a pumpkin muffin. Loaves of pumpkin bread cooled on the counter, together with a whole pumpkin waiting to be turned into tasty treats.

Well, t'was the season.

My gaze took in the stacks of bowls and cookie sheets on the counter and in the sink, then to the kitchen's focal point, the collection of cobalt bottles on the windowsill. Rays of sunshine danced off their surfaces, creating splashes of blue fire.

Holly, the black collie, sat herself at my feet, the best place to wait for a handout while Twister, the dark Belgian shepherd, lay in the doorway effectively blocking our exit. That was all right. Once settled in Camille's blue and white country kitchen, I was in no hurry to leave.

"Can you and Gilbert possibly eat all these baked goods?" I asked.

"Not and stay healthy. I give some to the neighbors and donate the surplus to the women's shelter in Maple Creek."

"I didn't know there was one."

"It's new. It's called the Oasis."

"That's a good idea." I remembered that Camille had once been in an abusive relationship. That was before she found the yellow Victorian, before she married Crane's uncle, Gilbert.

"Has anything exciting happened to you lately?" she asked.

"Lots of things." I told her about the Scarecrow House and the dozen scarecrows whose number had jumped to thirteen. "You can only see one of them from the road."

"That's unusual," she said. "Most farmers make do with one."

"I agree. Thirteen is overkill. I can't help wondering why that number." While we talked, I handed my cell phone to her, turned to the picture album.

She lingered on the last views I'd taken of the Adelaide in bridal white when she still wore her veil.

"Okay, this is beyond unusual," she said. "A wedding in a cornfield. Which one of these worthies is the groom?"

"Everyone is all dressed up. Who knows?"

"Maybe it's part of staging the house for sale," she said. "In which case, you don't have a mystery."

"Staging is usually done inside the house, though, isn't it? This would be curb appeal, except there's no curb on Mill Road, and you couldn't see behind the house anyway.

"There's something else at work here."

I added what I considered the heart of the story, the Scarecrow House and its mini me. Because I knew Camille wasn't a gossip, I mentioned Miss Eidt's unexpected reception of my gift.

"I always thought our librarian was the most open person I know," she said. "What do you suppose she's hiding?"

"It has to be more than a violent dislike of the house. But she isn't talking." Yet.

I would have to think of another way to find my answers.

"You girls have the best adventures," Camille said. "One of these days, I'll have to venture out of my kitchen."

"I'll take you to see the scarecrows," I said.

"I'd love that."

"Call me when you want to go."

She paused to brew the tea and move one of the pumpkin loaves to the table. "I think the real mystery is the bride. Why on earth dress a scarecrow in a bride's gown? And that dress had to be expensive."

"Maybe the owner thought white would scare the crows better than multi colors?"

"You'd think a flapping veil of any color would be sufficient to scare them away. I wonder where the veil is."

I decided I couldn't continue to keep Leonora's secret. "Leonora took it to keep it safe from the rain."

"She shouldn't have done that," Camille said.

"Well, no." I considered. I agreed with Camille but wondered what she meant. "Why do you say that?"

"She may have interfered with some plan."

I frowned. That sounded ominous. "What kind of plan?"

"We can't know. Or, looking at it another way, she broke a pattern."

"What pattern?"

"What was meant to be."

"I'll convince her to take it back," I said.

"That's best. Leave everything the way you found it."

For a moment, I might have been talking to Lucy.

Eleven

Some days, the devil himself slipped past the hall monitor and took up residence in my classroom. I estimated that seventy-five percent of the period was taken up with solving discipline problems, while in the remaining time I tried to teach the day's lesson.

Grimsley would take steps to remove me from the Marston faculty if he knew this.

I'd already learned that my first period freshman class was incorrigible. They couldn't possibly be louder. A pretty girl with a proliferation of blonde curls and the unflattering nickname of Chatty Catty screamed out her every utterance.

At the moment, she was screaming the answer to the first question on an impromptu quiz. I reached over her desk. "This isn't group work, Catherine. You just forfeited that item."

"What does that mean? Forfeit?"

"It isn't going to count."

"That's not fair," she cried.

"Cheating isn't fair either. Not to yourself, not to the rest of the class."

"Wait till my mother hears about this!"

Correction. Wait until her mother heard about her daughter's behavior. Unless she was one of those parents whose offspring could do no wrong.

Small wonder that by the end of the school day I looked forward to a nice fright-inducing mystery.

"Can I go to the bathroom?" Becky asked.

Losing the spotlight, Catty ended her tirade.

"Not until the quizzes are finished," I said.

The invisible devil in the corner smirked at me. "Carry on."

~ * ~

Tamryn Lynn lived in a light purple ranch house with black shutters on Chestnut Boulevard, which was more a lane than a boulevard. A three-branched tree grew in the front yard, one of whose branches leaned precariously on the roof. If this were my house, I wouldn't have a minute's peace in a thunderstorm or high wind.

Tamryn, however, appeared oblivious of imminent calamity. Her only concern was the return of Cara.

"I have a confession to make," she said as we strolled to the back yard, passing neatly kept flower beds. On three sides, they framed a velvety expanse of green lawn, except where the lilac grew, along with a pretty bushy tree. Tamryn identified it as a mock orange.

The lilac tree, alas, was on its way out. It looked like a bunch of dead branches put together in the general shape of a tree with an abandoned birds' nest at its top.

"What a shame," I said. "Your tree is dying."

Tamryn squinted into the sun. "It'll come back in the spring."

"If you say so."

"You should have seen how pretty Cara looked with the lilacs in the background. It's too bad lilac season is so short."

"I love them, too," I said.

She touched a dead branch fondly. "I'm thinking of adding some fall decor to the yard. Anything except pumpkins. Everybody has pumpkins."

"I saw some nice scarecrows at a house on Mill Road," I said. "I'm thinking of buying one."

"Mill Road, huh? I'll look into it."

I was happy to see her enthusiastic about something besides her dead collie. Then she said, "I haven't seen Cara in days. That's why I postponed your other visits."

"Maybe the phenomenon went away. That's good."

"Not really. Cara is still here. I can sense her. Sometimes, I hear her tags jingling, and a sigh that could only come from her."

She stared at the space in front of the dead tree...at its shadow...as if willing the shadow to reshape itself into a beloved collie.

"I know," she said. "I'll wrap a string of pumpkin lights around the lilac tree. Cara will be happy to see that."

Lights around a dead tree. Well, I suppose it would be different.

We were in an ordinary back yard with flowers and grass and no hint of anything off. Would Lucy Hazen look at this same scene and discern the secret beyond the ordinary?

"I have a friend..." I began.

Tamryn was obviously in a world of her own. She touched her necklace, a gold cross with a small sparkling stone in its center and continued to stare at the shadow.

At last she said, "Above all, I want Cara to come back. I have to know if she's happy being brought back to life, or if she'd rather return to the rainbow bridge."

Good grief. Tamryn was truly unbalanced if she believed what she was saying. I'd better find an excuse to decline her offer of refreshment and leave her to her delusion.

"If by chance she isn't happy, then I don't know how I can help her," she said. "I'd hate to have to kill her again."

How could I respond to that remark?

"Will you come again, Jennet?" she asked. "Sooner or later, I'm sure you'll be able to see her."

I didn't know how to refuse without letting her know that I had no faith in this particular ghost dog.

"Sometime," I said vaguely. "I'll see."

"I'd be so grateful if you would. I just wish you could stay longer today. Cara could still appear."

She stepped into the lilac tree's shadow and reached down as if to stroke a lying animal.

Her hand touched the grass.

"I have to go home and feed my dogs," I said. "I've been away all day. My husband gets angry if I don't serve his dinner on time."

Sorry, Crane.

I didn't think Tamryn cared if I went or stayed. Did I say I hadn't felt anything in Tamryn's yard? As I walked back to my car, a sensation of cold engulfed me. It had nothing to do with the imagined fragrance of lingering lilac blooms.

~ * ~

On the way home, I stopped at Sue's horse ranch, surprised to find eight collies at play. I counted them to be sure. Yes, eight. A new dog must have come into rescue.

Sue rose from the rocker on the porch to greet me. "Velvet came back."

"I thought you found the perfect home for her."

"So did I. The family returned her. They just said it didn't work out."

Velvet detached herself from the pack, and, tail wagging enthusiastically, ran up to me, raising her paw to shake hands. Who had taught her that trick?

"That's all they said? It didn't work out?"

"Not much of a reason, is it? Sort of like irreconcilable differences."

"What happened, girl?" I asked Velvet, looking into her dark, soulful eyes.

"I can't figure it out," Sue said. "She's gorgeous and sweet. Anyone who loves collies should fall in love with her at first sight."

"She seems happy with you."

"I can't keep all my rescues," Sue said. "Velvet likes you. After all, you rescued her."

"I have seven collies already, and an extremely tolerant husband," I reminded her.

And a demanding job and a large house to take care of. And an occasional mystery to solve. I let the subject of Velvet's ownership drift away and told her about my visit to Tamryn. "I can't help her, Sue. She's lost touch with reality."

"Are you going to see her again?" Sue asked.

"If she calls me, I suppose I'll go. But if she doesn't see Cara again, who knows?"

Sue said, "Maybe you should take Velvet with you the next time you visit Tamryn. If she could see her—"

"No," I said quickly. "That wouldn't be fair to Velvet. Tamryn is a loose cannon. We don't want to have Velvet known as the collie who can't find a home."

Velvet had rejoined the pack. They were racing around the corral chasing Bluebell who proudly held a rainbow-colored dragon in her mouth, the prize of the day.

"She'll stay with me for the time being," Sue said. "I'll see if I can detect any undesirable traits in her and work on them."

Being a dog, Velvet couldn't tell me why a home with a caring mother and two playful children hadn't worked out for her. Which left us with another mystery. Which left *Sue* with a mystery, I amended. I had Tamryn and Cara, and that situation had no easy solution.

Twelve

On returning home, I found Brent Fowler sitting in the rocking chair deep in conversation with Crane. They fell silent when I joined them, giving me cause to wonder if they were talking about me.

"Did you see Tamryn's ghost dog?" Crane asked.

"No, and I don't think there is one. Tamryn is more disturbed than we thought."

"What's this?" Brent asked. "You found another ghost?"

"Not exactly." I told him about Tamryn's obsession with the ashes of her departed collie, Cara.

"That's weird," Brent said. "Like something Stephen King would write. I have a pet cemetery out at the barn."

"Who died?"

"No one yet. I just set aside the land for when it's needed. Well, enough morbid stuff. I came to invite you and the sheriff here to have dinner with me at the Hunt Club Inn sometime soon."

"I'd love that," I said, envisioning prime rib with all the trimmings, none of which I'd have to cook.

I was already thinking about what I'd wear. My favorite red dress. I'd worn it to the Hunt Club Ball on my first fall in Foxglove Corners. It would look terrific with my crystal pendant and teardrop earrings.

Brent interrupted my woolgathering. "Good. Now what did you make for our dinner tonight?"

Our dinner?

"I haven't yet."

I rose, my thoughts spinning around possible menus. I had a large sirloin steak defrosting. That would be quick and easy. And these days, I always had an apple pie, which reminded me of the cider mill and scarecrows. Maybe Brent knew something about the scarecrows.

~ * ~

When I repeated the story of our adventure at the house on Mill Road, I didn't mention that Leonora had removed the veil, not wanting Brent to think she was a thief when her intention was to protect it from the rain.

It was raining now, strong drops pelting the windows. Sky left the circle of collies and, with a whimper, took refuge under the dining room table. There she was safe.

"Is that hail?" Crane asked, peering out the window.

"Sounds like it," Brent said, apparently not interested in the weather. "How do you manage to find the most bizarre places in Foxglove Corners, Jennet?"

"Innocently. Annica and I were en route to the Brightwater Cider Mill. Anyone could have discovered the scarecrows."

"Most people would drive right by the house and maybe comment about its gloomy appearance," Crane said. "Who but Jennet would stop? Why *did* you stop, by the way?"

"To satisfy my curiosity. I thought the miniature house I bought for Miss Eidt was inspired by Scarecrow House. And it was. It's a perfect imitation."

"That's bizarre, too," Brent said.

I agreed. "What can I say? One bizarre occurrence leads to another one." I held back Miss Eidt's odd reaction to my gift.

Brent's eyes sparkled. "That's it! My new enterprise."

"Are you referring to *my* mystery?" I asked.

"Sure. You don't own it, and I know just what I'm going to do."

Thunder rumbled overhead, and lightning streaked through the room. From her safe place, Sky wailed. Brent called her name. She tilted her head but didn't come to him.

"What?" I asked.

"You said the house is for sale. I'll pretend to be interested in it. While the realtor shows me the house, I'll ask about the scarecrows. There's probably a simple explanation."

"I said the house was vacant. I didn't see a 'For Sale' sign."

"Irrelevant. It'll be easy to find out who owns it."

"Your new enterprise may be short-lived," I said. "One question, one answer, and it's over."

"Maybe, but like you said, one bizarre happening leads to another."

My mind drifted to Tamryn's situation. She had scattered Cara's ashes in her back yard, which in itself was a common enough practice. That led to her belief that she had, thereby, brought Cara back to life. Which might lead her in any number of strange directions.

I wondered where the band of scarecrows would take me.

~ * ~

"I found another home for Velvet," Sue said as we sat on her porch the next day. "They fell in love with her. They're an active family, always hiking or camping, always on the go."

"Does Velvet like to hike?" I asked.

"We don't know what her first years were like."

At present, Velvet lay on the porch with Icy and Scarlet while the other dogs wandered aimlessly in the grass, sniffing at those mysterious scents discernible only to canines.

"The family, the Kimbroughs, lost one of their two collies recently. His companion is still mourning him."

"Let's hope they get along."

"Keep your fingers crossed. People don't usually return dogs they adopt, but occasionally it happens."

"Velvet is so beautiful. Who wouldn't want her?"

"She's sweet and laid back. I can't understand what went wrong with her other family."

A sinister buzzing insinuated itself into the lazy silence. Danger! Bee!

Velvet opened her eyes and fixed her eyes on the noisy insect. Scarlet sniffed the air, and I resisted the impulse to run back into the house, having once had a severe bee sting allergy. The bee, apparently aware of three sets of sharp teeth eager to end its life, took flight.

After a while, Sue asked, "What are we going to do about Tamryn?"

"There's nothing we can do. I'm hoping this delusion plays itself out."

"It's uncanny," Sue said. "Bringing a dead dog back to life. As if that could happen. I never scattered ashes," she added. "I keep them in a special container."

Tamryn and ashes were depressing subjects for a fine autumn afternoon. I laid my hand on Velvet's head, reveling in the soft warmth of her fur. The icy fingers of death seemed so far away it was almost possible to wish them out of existence.

"Good luck in your new home, Velvet," I said.

She flattened her ears and wagged her tail.

I could sit on Sue's porch all evening soaking up the last rays of sun, listening to the leaves wake and rustle at the touch of the wind. But real life called. I had my own collies to take care of, dinner to make, and a test to create for my English literature classes. I started to get up.

After a while, Sue said, "Tamryn wants to join the Rescue League."

"Are you going to let her?"

"How can I refuse? We're not an exclusive club. As long as she's interested in rescue and willing to volunteer her time and resources... Well, those are our requirements. Only—"

"Only?"

"This obsession of hers disturbs me," Sue said. "We want people who are normal to represent us. What if she tells one of our clients that she scattered her dog's ashes and brought her back to life? We'd lose our credibility."

"Give it some time," I suggested. "Maybe she won't see Cara again and will stop looking for her."

Good advice, but did I believe it? Not entirely. One doesn't give up an obsession so easily. Tamryn disturbed me, too. I didn't like feeling that way, but I did.

"I have to think about this long and hard," Sue said.

"I'll see you soon."

"Keep me in the loop," she said.

I rose. Velvet padded along beside me to the car. On some level, I was afraid she thought her home was with me.

Thirteen

Leonora looked pale and drawn when I picked her up the next morning. So much so that I asked, "Are you sure you want to go to school today? You don't look so good."

She dropped her books, her purse, and a package in the backseat. Even her blonde hair had lost its luster, and her bright red turtleneck sweater only emphasized her lack of color.

"I didn't get enough sleep last night," she said. "I hope the kids are on their best behavior."

It was Friday, a warm overcast fall day. I imagined several of our scholars, especially the seniors, would get together for an impromptu skip day. If by some miracle we teachers were granted a free day, I knew where I'd go. To the cider mill.

As if she had read my mind, Leonora said, "Could we drive out to the Scarecrow House after school?"

"Sure. But why?"

"It's this nightmare I had. It was so real. So horrible."

She shuddered. "I feel I need to do something about it."

Leonora rarely talked about her dreams. She claimed she didn't remember them and nobody was interested in hearing about another person's dreams, anyway.

"You couldn't sleep because of a dream?" I asked. "Maybe you're coming down with something."

"I don't think so. I don't have a temperature. But I feel like a dishrag."

"That bad, huh?"

"Worse."

We were traveling on one of those country roads lined with dark woods where the occasional Deer X-ing signs and absence of houses promised secrecy. *Whatever is said in the car stays in the car.*

"Let me tell you what I dreamed," she said. "Maybe then it'll lose its hold on me."

If retelling the dream didn't free Leonora from her present state, certainly her lively first period class would. I reminded her of that, sat back to watch the road, and listened.

"I was hanging on a pole behind the Scarecrow House," she said. "There was a storm. Lightning and thunder. The rain lashed at my body. I struggled but couldn't free myself. I tried to cry for help, but the only sound I could make was a croak."

"How ghastly! It *did* rain a little last night, around two o'clock, but I didn't hear any thunder."

"You're suggesting the real rain inspired the storm in my dream."

"Am I?"

She didn't answer but continued. "The other scarecrows came to life. They were dancing around me and chanting. One of them was the bride. She kept screaming at me to bring her veil back."

"Is that why you want to go back to the house?" I said. "To return the veil?"

"I have to."

"Is it in that package in the back?"

"Yes. When we get there, I'll put it on the bride's head. Then, I never want to see that place again."

"How could the scarecrows dance without feet?"

"It was a dream, Jennet. Strange things happen."

"Keep telling yourself that," I said. "Then you won't be afraid."

She snapped to attention. "I'm not afraid. I...I just don't feel well. I need at least eight hours of sleep to function properly."

I did as well. A sleep-deprived teacher couldn't possibly keep up with a boisterous class or, better still, keep one step ahead of it. Especially these days with Grimsley hounding us about weekly progress reports.

"Try to take a nap now," I said. "You have at least a half hour."

"I'll try."

She closed her eyes, but as I entered the southbound freeway, she said, "What do you think Lucy Hazen would say about my dream?"

"That it was just a dream inspired by a truly strange sight. Then maybe you feel a little guilty about taking the veil."

"I do...now. I only thought what a waste it would be if the rain ruined it. I should have known I couldn't get away with it, with all those eyes watching me."

"What eyes?"

"Scarecrow eyes."

"They don't have eyes, Leonora," I said. "Their faces are canvas."

She didn't answer. Surely she wasn't serious.

After a moment, she said, "Maybe it's a sign."

"A sign of what?"

"I'm not sure. I'd really like to see what Lucy makes of it."

"We can do that," I said.

Perhaps it would be a good idea to ask for Lucy's input unless Leonora's concern ended when she returned the veil. I hoped that would be the case.

~ * ~

It was drizzling with a fitful wind when I pulled into the broken concrete driveway of the Scarecrow House. Dark deserted house, gray sky, an atmosphere so thick you could cut it with a pair of scissors. And behind the house an encroaching horror.

Uh-oh. I sounded like Leonora.

Leonora had unwrapped the veil and let it lie in her lap, still folded, as if loath to touch it until she had no other choice.

In my opinion, she looked worse than she had this morning, although she had attempted to compensate for her pasty complexion by applying a coat of dark red lipstick.

"Do you want to stay inside the car while I return the veil?" I asked.

"No. I have to do this myself."

"I'll go with you then."

I grabbed my purse out of habit but left the key in the ignition. In case we had to get away in a hurry?

Ridiculous. The house was empty, and there was no one in sight nor any traffic. What we had to do would take about five minutes' travel time—to the scarecrow field and back. We wouldn't even have to time to get wet.

"Let's hurry," I said, stepping out of the car.

Well, we were getting a little wet. There were degrees of drizzle and the wind insisted on blowing water into our faces. In addition, the grass on this side of the house was sparse and the ground muddy.

Leonora reached the back of the house first and stopped so abruptly I almost ran into her. "What on earth?" she murmured.

"What...?

But I saw it. Or rather I saw the space where Adelaide the bride had stood, easily distinguished from the scarecrow family by her long white bridal gown.

She was gone.

"There are only twelve of them now," Leonora said. "What happened?"

"There were twelve when I first saw them. Someone may have taken one of them down, probably the same person who put it up."

"But why?"

"I can't imagine. Maybe he thought the bride looked incomplete without her veil."

My explanation didn't seem likely to me. If that were the case, though, wouldn't a white scarf or even a piece cut from a sheet serve as a makeshift bridal veil? These were, after all, only scarecrows, not fashion models.

I walked over to examine the site, the place where the thirteenth scarecrow had been installed. Someone—perhaps a perfectionist?—had taken care to rake dirt over the impression made in the ground by the pole. To make it look as if it had never been there.

"If you hadn't seen the scarecrow, too, I'd think I dreamed it," I said.

"It was definitely there."

"Okay, where is it now?" she asked.

It hardly mattered. "In the garage or barn. Maybe in the house."

Leonora shivered. The drizzle had turned into a steady rain in a matter of minutes. "Now what do I do with the veil?"

It hung freely from her hand, touching the ground, getting dirty in spite of her initial resolve to keep it clean.

"Let's see. You could leave it on the back porch. Or...I know. Just drape it around one of the other scarecrows. How about taking off Maisie's hat and putting the veil on her head?"

"And what would we do with the hat?"

"We put the hat back on over the veil."

"Let's do it then, and get out of here," she said.

Leonora practically threw the veil over the straw-haired head. Then I topped it with the garish hat and we were through.

"The veil got wet anyway," I said. "Wet and dirty."

"This is the best I could do," she said, appearing to address the missing bride. "I'm sorry. Forget this ever happened."

I started to remind Leonora that the scarecrows were things, not people, but what was the point? We both knew they were made of straw and dressed in rather nice clothes, utterly insentient. And now, the weird episode was concluded.

Fourteen

The rain continued. I listened to the hypnotic swish of the windshield wipers andlonged for home and a cup of hot tea.

Relieved of her burden, Leonora lay her head back against the seat as I steered out to the road. "Well, that's done," she murmured.

"Now you can forget about it."

"I hope."

"You don't have any reason to come back this way."

"No—"

But *I* did. The other mystery, Miss Eidt and the miniature house, was alive and well.

Leonora didn't need to be a part of it.

Belatedly, I asked, "How did your day go?"

"Not good. With most classes, you have to be right out there with them. I couldn't find the energy to do that today, so I revised my plans a little and gave them busy work. Wouldn't you know Grimsley chose today to spy on my World Lit class? He just walked in, sat in an empty seat and watched them answer questions from the book, then left without saying a word."

"That's how he operates," I said, having been on the receiving end of a surprise visit last year. "He may never say a word about it, leaving you to wonder why he was there and what he thought."

"I can't worry about him now. I left emergency lesson plans in my folder in case I have to call in sick tomorrow."

"It's this weather," I said. "Chilly one day, warm the next."

And wet. I was driving slowly and carefully over a surface turned slippery with fallen leaves, barely able to see the road in front of me, but mindful of the Deer Crossing signs I knew were out there.

Any sensible deer is hunkered down in his thicket, I thought.

"Thanks for going with me today," Leonora said. "I'm going to call Lucy in a day or two. I'll see how I feel." She paused. "You'll come with me?"

"Of course, but you'll forget all about the Scarecrow Bride by then. An early night should erase that nightmare permanently.

"I don't think it's over. It may just be beginning."

"Let's hope you're wrong," I said.

~ * ~

Home at last, and thank heavens for the casserole I'd made last night. Crane was home before me which rarely happened. He had fed the dogs and must have walked them as they were still in play mode. He had also heated the casserole. I truly had the best of husbands. I dodged Misty's dancing paws to kiss him.

"Leonora wanted to take the veil back to the scarecrow field," I said. "But the bride was gone."

"What did you do?" he asked.

"Left it on another scarecrow. That's one of the creepiest places in Foxglove Corners."

I was happy to push it to the back of my mind. Another day, I'd take it out, scarecrows and all, and approach it from a different angle. Tonight I wanted to enjoy a hot dinner and a quiet evening at home with Crane. I wanted to read more of *Haldane Station*.

Instead, I found myself entertaining Brent Fowler who was eager to share his impressions of the Scarecrow House with us. We sat in the living room chatting over coffee and apple pie. Uncharacteristically, Brent had arrived too late to join us for dinner.

"Lucy and I drove out to see the house today," he said. "She thinks the scarecrows are clever, but she doesn't see a mystery there."

Lucy didn't know about the appearance and subsequent disappearance of the thirteenth scarecrow, nor of Leonora's appalling dream. I hadn't told her about my own impression either, about a sense of being watched from an empty house. Naturally, she would think the gathering of scarecrows was only a harmless curiosity.

For all I knew, that was all they were.

"I ran into a dead end trying to find out who owns the house," Brent said. "None of the local realtors is handling it."

"It isn't for sale then. Maybe it's somebody's country home, and they haven't furnished it yet."

"I tried to find a neighbor to ask. There's an old farmhouse a couple of miles down the road. It looked like it was deserted, too. No one was home in the other direction." He paused to pet Misty who had sidled up to him and uttered a pitiful little whimper. She didn't like to wait for attention.

"By the way," he said, "I counted eleven scarecrows. Didn't you say there were thirteen?"

"With the bride, there were."

"There are eleven now."

"What time were you there?" I asked.

"Around noon."

At noon, Leonora and I were at Marston High School eating lunch. We must have arrived at the house after three. I couldn't swear the bride was the only scarecrow missing. It had been raining; we'd been in a hurry. I remembered Leonora holding the veil, wondering where to leave it now that Adelaide was gone.

It hadn't occurred to me to count scarecrows. "I suppose you're certain," I said.

"Positive. Lucy was with me. She'll tell you."

"There's a simple explanation," Crane said. "They might be for sale, and the man who set them out sold two."

"Then wouldn't there be a sign visible from the road and prices posted? There's nothing like that. Just a diminishing number of scarecrows."

"Someone is playing musical scarecrows," Brent said.

"Where are the chairs?" Crane asked.

"Don't be so literal, Sheriff," Brent said. "I wonder. If you stop by tomorrow, will there be ten?"

I wondered, too, imagining the scarecrows vanishing one by one until a single bunch of hay dressed in somebody's Sunday best was left to guard the field.

"I'm not going to do that," I said.

Tomorrow I wanted to come home after school, unwind, and correct tests. Maybe I'd call Lucy. She didn't know the whole story. There was a mystery at Scarecrow House, but it would keep.

"I'll go then," Brent said.

~ * ~

The next day during my conference hour, I sat at my desk in my blessedly quiet classroom staring at a blank form. It was Friday, the day Grimsley's progress reports were due.

Leonora had dodged a bullet by taking another day off. She'd still have to turn in a report describing her progress, or, more likely, lack of progress when she came back.

I let my gaze roam around the room, which was in a bit of a shambles after five classes had squirmed in their desks and dropped debris on the floor. Fallen paper, an illegal candy bar, a tissue—a mess.

What had I done to improve the image of Marston High School this week? Oh, good grief.

I'd provided a neat, clean learning environment for my students. I eyed the discarded candy wrapper. In life, it had been an Almond Joy. How had its owner managed to devour it under my watchful eyes?

One surreptitious bite at a time while I was concentrating on someone else.

My students needed sugar to survive my English literature class. Okay. I let them eat candy in class in spite of the Rules.

Think! This is your ticket home.

I picked up my pen and let it hover above a blank space until inspiration struck.

In two classes, I had assigned them to choose one of Chaucer's pilgrims and tell his or her story to the class using modern day English.

Incidentally, I should do that. Would Grimsley be impressed? Hardly. But it was something to write in that aggravating blank space. Now, what did I do in my other classes? A variation on the theme?

Hastily, I scribbled a few sentences, gathered the books I was going to take home and waited for the bell. I was driving back to Foxglove Corners alone today and expected the ride to be twice as long.

<h1 style="text-align:center">Fifteen</h1>

I was dreaming about scarecrows, which wasn't surprising, given recent events. What was surprising was their location...my classroom at Marston High School. They sat in the desks, thirteen of them, heads without human features, faces without eyes. Strands of straw drifted down from their bodies, littering the floor.

Where were my second period seniors? How could I teach Chaucer's poetry to insentient bunches of straw?

Grimsley burst into the room, a paper clutched in his hand. His characteristic pasted-on smile had turned into a mask of rage.

"You dare to mock me by submitting this trash?" he demanded.

That was my report in his hand. He waved it in my face, then tossed it into the wastebasket.

"I guess I do," I said, trying to keep my voice from quivering.

"Off with her head!" he shouted.

The scarecrows found their voices. Cheers erupted from the class. They rose and silently advanced on me. Dust from their straw bodies flew through the air, choking me.

The bride led two of her fellows to the front of the class. They took their stand behind me. Grimsley blocked the door. I was surrounded. There was no way to escape.

Except to wake up.

I opened my eyes. Bright moonlight streamed through the windows, and shadows lay motionless throughout the room.

Oh, dear Lord. What mix of innocuous images had produced that horror?

I ran my fingers along my throat. At least I still had my head. But my nightgown was soaked with perspiration. My heartbeat was erratic and my mouth was as dry as…well, as dry as straw. I could swear that a strand of straw was caught in my tooth. Maybe it was a dog hair.

Crane slept on, but at some point, Misty had left Halley and their chosen sleeping place in the doorway to sit by my side of the bed. She nudged my arm.

Are you all right?

"Go back to sleep, baby," I whispered, but she didn't move, even when I left the bed and walked quietly over to the dresser for a fresh nightgown.

It was only two-thirty. There was plenty of the night left.

And please, Lord, don't send me another nightmare.

~ * ~

Morning sunlight stole over the countryside as I drove out to Jonquil Lane the next day. After yesterday's rain, the landscape fairly glittered. It was going to be unseasonably warm.

What is so rare as a day in October?

Plans, I decided, were meant to be broken. Last night, weary and shivery after our detour to the scarecrow field, nothing had seemed more appealing than an early night unless it were a fresh load of apples.

I would have extra time today as Leonora had called in sick again. I couldn't think of anything better to do than take another trip to the cider mill.

A single cloud drifted across my mind, a half-remembered dream. Something about scarecrows, something vaguely disturbing. I didn't make an attempt to remember it but concentrated on driving and admiring the scenery, waving leaves fashioned of fire against a pure blue sky.

But I missed Leonora. If I were going to have an adventure this afternoon, I wanted her to be with me.

~ * ~

By ten o'clock, the day already showed signs of being a good one. Leonora's classes in the room next to mine roared on as if they were filled with maddened zoo creatures. I introduced my Chaucer Characters lesson to my English literature students, and let them choose their pilgrim, and begin jotting down notes to aid them in bringing the characters to life.

It went well. At lunch, I checked my mail box. I had a note from the principal's office.

Uh-oh. I unfolded it and read:

Mrs. Ferguson, Your idea (Progress Report #1) is innovative and creative. Exactly what I'm looking for. Please invite me to your class when the speeches begin.

I nearly dropped the note, remembering how I'd agonized over what to write. What was rarer than a compliment from Principal Grimsley?

But...Did I have to write one of these every week? Could I come up with a new plan before leaving the school next Friday? I'd just used my only idea.

And now I'd have to invite him to my class.

Don't think about that, I chided myself. *Enjoy the moment.*

The rest of my classes were uneventful, even enjoyable. When the last bell rang, I set out for the Brightwater Cider Mill. I'd added a pound of maple walnut fudge to my shopping list for a well-deserved reward.

~ * ~

Before I left the school parking lot, I sent Brent a text message, asking him if he'd visited the scarecrows today as planned. He had and there were still eleven of them. I had no reason to stop at Scarecrow House myself today, but I was driving past it and could spare the time. I could count straw bodies and see who was missing besides the bride.

The house presented its usual dour facade to the road. Last night's wind had stripped more leaves from the trees, giving me a rustling carpet to tread upon. I walked around to the back of the house and surveyed the scarecrow family. There were eleven, as Brent had informed me, but one of them was new. Harvey, or Dracula, the scariest of the scary, was missing. Or perhaps I was looking at Dracula in a new outfit. How could you tell with eleven identical bodies of straw? I'd only identified Dracula because of his long cape.

Another scarecrow, Imogen, lay face down in the dirt.

Face down? Why did I persist in speaking of them in human terms? The wind had probably knocked Imogen down, although all of the scarecrows had seemed secure on their poles.

I tried to lift her, but she was heavier than she looked and about four inches taller than I was. Something sharp scraped against my hand and I let the straw person fall back on the ground. I saw then that she wore a large medallion on a long chain, an accessory, like the others too expensive for a scarecrow.

I had the oddest sense that someone was watching me, waiting for me to make a wrong move. Perhaps the watcher spied on my activities from behind the bare windows?

But no. I couldn't see a face and there were no curtains to move back at a surreptitious touch.

Still, I'd better be on my way. If only I could figure what was going on at Scarecrow House. And one more question arose. Granted, the house was in an isolated area, but surely I wasn't the only person who had seen the scarecrows. Why were they still wearing their expensive clothing and jewelry like Imogen's medallion? One would think by now a vagrant would have discovered the treasure trove and stolen the pricey accessories.

With my question unanswered, I hurried back to my car. I was eager to hear Brent's thoughts on the subject and anxious to put distance between me and Scarecrow House.

~ * ~

My phone rang twice in my purse while I was driving. I never answer it until I reach my destination. In my own driveway, a half hour later, I saw that Sue Appleton was trying to call me, which usually meant the Rescue League had a pressing problem.

She came right to the point. "It's Velvet. Her new family, the

Kimbroughs, wants to try adoption again with a different dog."

Oh, no.

I thought of Velvet as I'd last seen her—so beautiful, so happy, padding along beside me as I walked to the car. Without knowing any of the details of her rejection, my heart broke for her.

"What happened?" I asked.

"They claim she barks too much."

"*Hark, hark, the dogs do bark*," I murmured. "Velvet is a collie. She's vocal. Of course she barks."

"You'll remember this isn't their first collie. They say her barking is excessive. And they have neighbors. One lady is tired of waking up to barking in the middle of the night."

"Surely that's an exaggeration."

"She's retired. She sleeps in every morning, or tries to."

"There must be something the Kimbroughs can do other than surrender her," I said.

"They're adamant. They want to return Velvet to us and choose another collie."

"And they think that dog won't bark?"

"Not excessively, or so they hope. Velvet has stayed with me for a while now. I didn't notice she was noisier than any of my other collies. Mrs. Kimbrough says she mostly barks at people walking their dogs and there are a lot of dog walkers in her neighborhood. Besides, their other collie doesn't like her."

"Are you going to take her back?" I asked.

"Definitely. I'd never leave a dog with a person who doesn't want her."

"Will you give them another collie?"

"We have others to place. I can't see alienating prospective owners."

"Poor Velvet. It isn't fair to her."

"I'll find her a new home, but I thought this was the one."

"I hope the next one will be," I said. "Keep me informed."

Leaving the apples for Crane to carry in to the house, I took the fudge and caramel apples inside. Knowing that Velvet had lost her latest home marred the perfection of the day.

Sixteen

After school the next day, Leonora and I took a detour to Lucy's atmospheric house on Spruce Road.

Leonora said, "I can't stop thinking about scarecrows. I had that dream again where I'm hanging on a pole and they're dancing around me."

"That's unusual. To have the same dream twice."

"It's downright uncanny."

"I dreamed about them, too," I said, "but I don't remember the details. I don't think they were moving."

I frowned, recalling Principal Grimsley's pronouncement. "Off with her head!" How different from his note of praise for my week's goal. A brief image of advancing scarecrows surfaced.

I was wrong. They were moving. In my dream.

"Remember," I said. "Lucy doesn't interpret dreams."

"I'll feel better after we talk to her," she said.

Lucy was waiting for us with Sky, at the end of the long, shaded drive. She'd been picking wildflowers. Sky bounded out to greet us, barking happily. Like most collies, she loved company and Lucy led a solitary life, happy enough roaming through the worlds she created. We were Sky's diversion.

"Come in and we'll dissect the scarecrows," Lucy said.

Dissect? I thought of straw dust and more of my dream came back to me. Scarecrows sitting in student desks shedding minute bits of straw. An insentient class in rebellion.

Following Sky, we trooped through the dark rooms to the heart of the house, the sun room, where Lucy cultivated green plants in all seasons and wrote her stories. She had laid the wicker coffee table with cups and saucers, white without a single decoration to obscure the tea leaf formations.

"Brent told me you didn't find anything suspicious about the scarecrows," I said.

"He's half right. After we left, I couldn't get them out of my mind, so I went back later alone. This time I sensed something off."

"I told you so," Leonora murmured.

"Can you be more specific?"

"I wish I could. I had a strong sense of waiting. Something is going to happen there soon. My advice to you, Leonora, is to stay away from that place. In a way I can't yet explain, it's going to target you or Jennet. Maybe it already has."

"Yikes," Leonora said. "I was counting on feeling better after I discussed them with you. I didn't even tell you about my nightmares yet."

I listened while she described hanging on a pole at the mercy of a thunderstorm and a band of scarecrows.

"I've had the same dream twice. Thankfully, I wake up before anything terrible happens."

"Being strung up on a pole seems terrible to me," I said.

The teakettle whistled, and Lucy rose. From the kitchen she said, "Your subconscious is warning you about the danger you could be in."

"From bunches of dressed-up straw?" I asked.

"From the Evil that conceived and guides them."

"If I don't go back to that place, will I be safe?" Leonora asked.

"Safer." Lucy accented the second syllable. "I can't imagine a scarecrow traveling across miles to get to you."

"What about me?" I asked. "Am I in danger, too?"

"Not so much."

"Why? What's different about me?"

"You're stronger than Leonora. They may not want to tangle with you."

Scarecrows?

I should be flattered but I couldn't help thinking that Lucy had gone overboard on the subject. Scarecrows were, after all, made of straw. They weren't human and weren't dangerous. Only in dreams.

We drank our tea and entertained Lucy with tales from Marston High School. She then read our tea leaves. We had good cups with no alarming symbols which cheered Leonora immensely. She considered herself out of the woods, so to speak.

For me, Lucy's impression of the scarecrows was a matter to take seriously. I was more than ready to meet the scarecrow challenge head-on and investigate the evil Lucy talked about. In my opinion, it was a legitimate part of the mystery.

~ * ~

Phone calls from Sue Appleton often brought disturbing news. This one concerned Velvet, who had escaped from her third home when a neighborhood child left the gate to the fenced yard open. Miraculously, in true Lassie fashion, she had covered the thirty miles back to Squill Lane, and Sue's horse farm. Home.

She arrived in one piece, her coat a mud-splattered, burr-encrusted nightmare, her eyes bright with pride at her achievement. She was hungry. On the day of her return, she ate three dinners.

Her latest owner, Mrs. Ludcroft, didn't want her back. "If she doesn't want us, we don't want her," she'd said, which was, in my opinion, an odd approach to take. Obviously the Ludcrofts hadn't wanted Velvet in the first place. I imagined they hadn't made her feel welcome and secure.

"So I have her back," Sue said. "I'm beginning to see the writing on the wall."

"Meaning?"

"Velvet is determined to be in charge of her own destiny. I've never placed a collie who didn't adjust to a new home happily."

"Are you going to keep her?"

"I can't and be fair to my other dogs. Not to mention the constant stream of rescues that pass through here. I'll keep trying to place her. Surely she won't reject every home I find for her."

"She might. You used the correct word. Determined."

"Would you consider adopting her?" Sue asked.

"I love tris, but seven is my limit."

Still, I couldn't help thinking that Velvet had chosen me that day at the Apple Fair when I had lured her to my car with a bear claw. Poor lost girl. She couldn't know I was going to pass her on to Sue.

Almost without realizing what I was doing, I let myself contemplate a household that included Velvet. In this vision of the future, Crane was agreeable to increasing our pack. But all of our collies were house dogs. We weren't set up to be a kennel.

No. Quit dreaming.

Somewhere there must be a home that was incomplete without a sweet, loyal collie in the family. Possibly the people who lived in that home didn't know what they were missing, but once they opened their door to Velvet, they would never look back. Their gate could be left open all day and Velvet wouldn't be tempted to go through it because she was finally where she was meant to be. She was their dog.

I firmly believed that family existed. If anyone could find them, that person was Sue Appleton.

~ * ~

That night, I dreamed about scarecrows again, but they weren't sitting in desks in my classroom. They were living in Scarecrow House which was filled with dusty, old-fashioned furniture. I saw them clearly as, silent and invisible, I moved through the rooms.

One, wearing a red apron, was stationed at the stove. She had just taken a cake out of the oven. It looked as if it were made of straw. Dracula in his cape stood in the living room in front of the fireplace reading a book. He wore sunglasses.

Another blocked access to the front door. I had the distinct impression that he could see me, which wasn't supposed to happen. Still another scarecrow leaned on the windowsill looking out at the road.

Strangely, they weren't threatening. On the contrary. They reminded me of the figures in Miss Eidt's dollhouse, much magnified, dressed in their Sunday best, unable to move of their own volition, and, therefore, harmless.

Except, where were the others? There should be thirteen or twelve. Or eleven. I wasn't sure anymore.

Then from different parts of the house, ominous rustling sounds broke the silence. Scarecrows on the move? Tramping over crusty leaves?

There's danger here. Leave now!

At that moment of enlightenment, the dream ended. I woke safe in bed, lying next to Crane, with Halley and Misty in the doorway guarding the room.

It wasn't a full-fledged nightmare, only odd. But I was afraid.

Seventeen

I didn't think I would hear from Tamryn Lynn again. Thoroughly immersed in the scarecrow mystery, I had stopped thinking about her belief that she had brought her dog back to life. In truth, I didn't want to deal with an unbalanced person or her delusion. However, when she contacted me the next day inviting me to her back yard to see her girl, I didn't have the heart to refuse.

"Cara is back," she said. "I saw her yesterday in the same place, lying under the lilac tree. She stayed longer this time, and when I talked to her, she heard me. I'm sure of it. She tilted her head and looked straight at me. I asked her if she was happy."

"How did she react?" I asked.

"She barked a few times, but when I called her to come, she didn't move."

Strange behavior for a beloved pet; for an illusion or a ghost, not so strange.

'What happened then?"

"After a while, she faded away. I really want you to see her. Will you come?"

I sighed, longing to say I was busy for the foreseeable future, but that would be unkind, even if stated in more palatable terms. I might as well humor her...one more time.

"When?"

"Tomorrow? She already came and left today. She only comes once a day, I think."

"Okay," I said. "Tomorrow after school."

"Last night I filled her bowl with water and left it near the lilac tree," she said. "This morning the bowl was empty."

I could think of any number of nocturnal rovers who might have drunk Cara's water. A deer, an opossum, a rat, another dog...

"That's proof," Tamryn said. "Don't you think so?"

"I don't know. Maybe a thirsty groundhog stopped by."

"I think it was Cara. Next, I'm going to leave out her food."

Oh, for goodness sake. That bowl would be empty in the morning, too. All it proved was that all God's creatures are hungry and thirsty.

"I'll see you tomorrow, Tamryn," I said. "But I can't stay long."

There. I'd established my way out. I'd go and wouldn't see Cara, then I'd leave. I wasn't fabricating an excuse. It would be based in fact. The hours after school were short and packed with chores.

"You're a good friend, Jennet," Tamryn said. "I can't tell you how much I appreciate what you're doing for me."

~ * ~

Cara didn't appear. Of course she didn't.

Tamryn refused to be discouraged. "I think maybe it's because of you, Jennet. She didn't know you before she died. She was always slow to warm up to new people."

"You could be right," I said.

I waited a respectable amount of time, admiring her neat flower beds, learning that Cara had helped her pull weeds, which amounted to digging holes, and finally I consulted my watch. "I might as well go home. She's obviously not going to show up tonight."

"It doesn't look like it. May I offer you some refreshment? Coffee or tea, and I have a strawberry cake."

"If it's okay, I'll take a rain check," I said.

"Oh, yes. I remember your husband gets upset if his dinner is delayed."

"Oh, right. He does." I'd almost forgotten my little white lie.

"I don't want to cause you trouble," she added.

I felt guilty, although why I should was a mystery. I'd done what Tamryn had asked of me. It hadn't turned out happily. How could it? But that wasn't my fault.

Still the light in her eyes had dimmed. At the same time, an odd premonition tugged at me. What if this were the last time I saw Tamryn? Could I have done more to help her come to grips with her bizarre dilemma?

Unlikely. What else could I possibly do? Furthermore, she didn't think of Cara's return as a dilemma. She had faith that she'd accomplished a miracle. Cara would return tomorrow. Tamryn would still leave her food dish out and, when the kibble was eaten during the night, she would think she'd fed Cara.

Accepting reality would no doubt be traumatic for her.

Tamryn was loath to let me go. "I'm so grateful that I have Cara that I want to pay it forward, so to speak."

I had to ask. "In what way?"

"I want to be a part of your rescue league. I can give your name as a reference, can't I?"

I wished I were already out the door on my way to the car. On the one hand, I didn't want to be unkind. On the other, I couldn't imagine Tamryn representing us.

"We haven't known each other that long. Perhaps one of your other friends—"

"Oh, but I feel close to you," she said. "You've been so kind."

I had to discourage her. "There's a lot of work involved in rescue. It isn't always Lassie who needs help. It's never glamorous. You may come across a dog with fleas or one who's been so abused he bites. Or he may be rabid."

"I know all that," Tamryn said. "I can do it all. If I thought I couldn't, I wouldn't consider joining Rescue. So will you help me?"

I felt as if she had pushed me to a cliff's edge and was just waiting to give me the final shove. What could I say?

"I'll do what I can."

"Good. I knew I could count on you. And Jennet, please understand about Cara. She really is here. She just didn't show herself to you. Be patient."

"I'll say goodbye then," I said, thinking how awkward that sounded. I added, "I've left my own dogs alone too long."

No need to tell her that Crane was home by then.

She walked me to my car. "Thank you for coming, Jennet," she said. "You're a good friend. Thank you for everything."

~ * ~

The visit left a bad taste in my mouth. Back home, making dinner while Candy waited patiently for me to drop a tasty morsel, I decided I had to extricate myself from the situation. I was out of my league. If Tamryn were to abandon her dark fantasy, she needed the guidance of a professional.

"I scattered my dead dog's ashes in the backyard and brought her back to life." How weird was that?

For her, Cara came and went like a dark wraith. She didn't act like a real dog. What dog wouldn't come when called by a beloved lost mistress from whom she had been separated?

Why couldn't Tamryn see that? Because she didn't want to.

If she were to ask me to view Cara's next appearance, all I had to do was remind her of what she had said, that Cara wouldn't show herself because of me.

That decided, I resumed cutting potatoes into small cubes to join the meat I was cooking for a stew.

My life was difficult enough these days without dealing with somebody else's illusion. The new watchword was Simplicity.

While the stew bubbled merrily on the stove, I turned the pages of the *Banner,* idly skimming over stories that didn't interest me. A large ad on the Entertainment page caught my attention:

Custom Scarecrows created by Gwendolyn Larkin
$75-$100
Order your scarecrow today
15 South Pine Road

A local phone number accompanied the ad.

Could the mysteries be so easily explained? The scarecrows were samples created by Gwendolyn to display her work.

Not so fast.

Why leave them on the property of an abandoned house? What was to stop an unscrupulous scarecrow lover from absconding with Maisie or Dracula?

Nothing.

Leonora and I had trespassed on the grounds with impunity.

The scarecrows' owner must make periodic visits to her display. She'd have taken/sold two of the thirteen scarecrows. She knew when the bridal veil disappeared and when it had been replaced on the wrong scarecrow. No mystery there.

But how to account for Leonora's horrid dreams? And my own?

A dream is only a dream.

Possibly some people feared scarecrows like others fear clowns. I'd never given the matter a thought. To me, scarecrows were simply farmers' helpers or autumn decorations.

Suddenly I knew what my next purchase would be.

~ * ~

"We already have a nice scarecrow," Crane said. "I stored it in the basement."

"Now we'll have two. This is my first real clue."

He sat in his chair at the dining room table. Candy, apparently thinking herself invisible, sat beside him. I shooed her away lest she leap on the table and gobble up the stew.

"That solves the mystery of the scarecrows then," he said. "Good work, honey."

"Sort of. I still wonder about the little house I gave Miss Eidt. Why is it a miniature duplicate of the actual house?"

"Some people have more than one talent," Crane pointed out. "Maybe the scarecrow maker is the person who carved the house. She might have lived there at one time."

"Gwendolyn Larkin," I said. "The name is familiar."

"There are a lot of Larkins in Foxglove Corners. Remember the man who gave tours of decorated houses at Christmastime?"

"Oh yes. His niece made our scarecrow."

"This lady may be another one of his nieces."

"It's exciting to have this lead," I said. "I'm going to call her tomorrow."

Unlike Crane, I didn't believe the mystery was solved. It was only the virtual tip of the iceberg. In a way, I was ambivalent about having the scarecrows' existence so easily explained. It was something of a letdown. How much better it was to think of them in their new attire guarding some dangerous secret.

Well, there was still the miniature house. As we ate, I began to plan my next move.

Eighteen

On Saturday, I gathered the last of the apples for my pie. They had vanished as if by magic, an entire bushelful, but then, both Crane and I had been snacking on them. Candy had developed a taste for the sweet, juicy fruit...as long as it was peeled and pared for her. I would have to go back to the cider mill soon, which meant passing Scarecrow House again.

My plan to purchase a scarecrow from Gwendolyn Larkin was on hold as I hadn't been able to contact her. Why would she include a phone number in an ad if she didn't intend to respond to inquiries? I'd left her a half dozen voice mails but was still waiting for an answer.

Oh well, from now on I'd concentrate on another aspect of my many-faceted autumn mystery, the miniature version of Scarecrow House. This would include a visit to the library, which, in any event, was a perfect way to while away a weekend afternoon. I still hoped to learn the source of Miss Eidt's indifference—or should I say aversion?—to my gift.

With two pies set far back on the counter to cool, and the dogs resting from their first walk of the day, I set out for the library, first stopping at the Hometown Bakery for a Saturday afternoon treat.

From her favorite chair on the porch, Blackberrry followed me with her jewel-eyed gaze, but didn't move a muscle as I walked past her, crunching down leaves.

"Carry on, Cat," I said and entered the library.

I found Miss Eidt adding paperbacks to the Gothic Nook. The library was crowded, mostly with teens and children, but strangely, Miss Eidt and I were the only ones in the Nook.

She always looked so neat and serene. In her powder blue shirtwaist dress and pearl choker, she reminded me of a gracious lady in an English manor house always ready with a welcome for a guest.

The Gothic Nook issued its own silent welcome. Every antique side table held candy dishes of covered chocolates interspersed with fanciful Halloween decorations.

I didn't see the miniature house anywhere. Did I really expect Miss Eidt to display it?

I helped myself to a chocolate cherry and set the bakery box on the table.

"Good morning, Jennet," she said. "Or is it afternoon already? Time flies when you're having fun. What's in the box?" she added.

"Assorted pastries."

"Marvelous. Just what I was wishing for."

She handed me a dog-eared paperback, *On the Night of the Seventh Moon*. "This looks good, doesn't it? Somebody was a Victoria Holt fan. Debbie found about a dozen of her books at an estate sale yesterday."

"I'm a fan, too." I perused the cover and read the summary on the back. "Is it okay if I take this one?"

"Be my guest. I'll read it when you finish."

She shelved the last book. "Let's have tea and open that box. I need a double dose of sugar."

The little house wasn't in her office either. Probably, it still languished in the cupboard, out of sight.

While she brewed the tea, I told her what I'd discovered about the scarecrows and my intent to add one to my skimpy fall decor.

"If they're for sale, I should buy one, too," she said. "For the Halloween party."

"You already have so many decorations."

"Except for the dollhouse, they're all small and ordinary. Pumpkins and paper cut-outs. If I can have a custom-made scarecrow, I'll order one in a costume. A spaceman. No, maybe a ghoul. Or a witch. She can act as hostess."

"We'll have to locate Ms. Larkin first."

"I'll let you do that," she said. "Call me when you find her."

I agreed to that. While we drank our tea, we talked about the coming party, about refreshments and whether or not it should be open house or invitation only. Afterward, with nothing decided, I took my Victoria Holt book, and walked back to my car, kicking leaves idly, watching them scatter in my path. A delicious scent rode the air, a heady mix of smoke and something nostalgic and pleasant. Peppermint? I knew Debbie had planted peppermint and spearmint in the library's backyard.

As I drove home, I thought about scarecrows. Every now and then Miss Eidt surprised me. Today marked the first time she had showed interest in anything connected with Scarecrow House.

And why was that?

She wasn't talking.

Don't look for further mysteries, I told myself. Miss Eidt had stated her reason and it was only natural for her to want a costumed scarecrow for her party.

By the time I reached Jonquil Lane, the fair weather had given way to an impending storm. The sky had darkened and the wind gathered strength. A few raindrops began to fall as I left the car.

Inside, the collies gathered around me, happy with wagging tails, except for Sky, who had taken refuge under the dining room table to wait out the storm. With two hours before Crane would be home, I gave them their treats, taking Sky her biscuit and settled myself in the rocker. Ah, weekends, a warm, dry house safe from the elements, and time.

Before opening my book, I tried Gwendolyn Larkin's number again, telling her she now had two customers for her scarecrows. Another voice mail. Why didn't she return my messages?

Shrugging, I opened my book and promptly fell under the spell of Victoria Holt's misty, magical Black Forest adventure. An hour passed, then two. The rain continued. The house was too quiet. Even the dogs were still.

The silence communicated a vague sense of unease. I should turn on the television or the CD player. A bit of Copland, maybe the waltz from *Billy the Kid,* would dispel the mood that had crept up on me.

I would. In a minute. I closed my eyes. Just for a minute. Lulled by the falling rain, I felt myself drifting away, not hearing the clock chime the next hour.

~ * ~

The cell phone's melodious notes rippled through my dreams. My book had fallen on Misty who, oblivious, slept at my feet.

Where was that phone?

In my purse, in the kitchen. It was still ringing when I retrieved it. A familiar name flashed up at me: Elizabeth Eidt. What on earth?

"Hello, Miss Eidt," I said.

Her voice was higher than usual, her words rushed. "Jennet! Thank God you're home. I need help—now."

"What's wrong?"

"I can't go into it over the phone, but could you come...and hurry. Please."

"To the library?" I asked

"No, to that house on Mill Road with the scarecrows. Something happened. I'm afraid and I don't know what to do."

Being a member of the Collie Rescue League, I was used to urgent summonses and the need to act immediately.

But Miss Eidt? I could hardly imagine her outside the quiet, orderly library, handing me an estate sale find or a cup of tea. Especially, I couldn't envision her at Scarecrow House.

"I'll be right there," I said with a quick glance at the clock, then out the window. The rain had tapered down to a drizzle.

I wrote a note for Crane and grabbed my raincoat. Once more, it was Jennet to the rescue.

Nineteen

The storm must have been more severe in the Mill Road area. The pavement was wet and slick, branches littered the road, and I chafed at the slow speed I was forced to drive. The urgency in Miss Eidt's voice had affected me.

Hurry, hurry, the windshield wipers seemed to say as they kept the glass clear of raindrops falling from the trees.

Something had happened. I couldn't imagine what, but it was bad.

At last Scarecrow House appeared, swimming out of a light mist. Gables clean-washed and darkly shining, grass hidden under a new layer of autumn leaves, a bright blue Camry—blue was Miss Eidt's favorite color—parked in the broken concrete drive. Her new car but no other vehicle. The place was still vacant and forbidding.

Miss Eidt huddled on the porch, her beige raincoat resting on her shoulders, a rose patterned scarf lying untied against her blue shirtwaist dress. She must have driven here straight from the library without stopping at home. But why?

I'd soon know.

I parked behind the Camry. She came down the stairs to meet me, holding onto the rail for support.

"Oh, thank God, Jennet. I thought you'd never get here."

I hadn't wasted a minute, but at present that was irrelevant.

"What's the matter?" I asked. "Why are you here of all places?'

"I came to look at the scarecrows. You know, for the party." She hooked her fingers in the choker necklace as if it were indeed choking her. "I found...Well, come with me. You'll see."

She walked unsteadily around the house as if suddenly weak. I took her arm and we reached the back and the scarecrows. They, too, had a fresh-washed look. One had fallen over. Dracula? A black cloak pooled around his lower body.

I looked again. It wasn't straw that lay under the cape. It was flesh. A head, a neck, a mass of black hair. A chest drowned in blood.

Nausea washed over me in waves. I swallowed.

At my side, Miss Eidt was shaking. "Do you see?"

I took a few steps, stopped. "What happened?"

"I found him like this. He's dead."

Unmindful of the damp ground, I knelt beside the body. The man lay on his back, one arm at an awkward angle, his hand resting on the cape. His eyes were open, staring at nothing, all the vital force drained out of them.

Oh, yes, he was dead. Who could live with the blood drained out of him?

Dracula—

I felt like rushing away from the scarecrow field, back to my cozy, safe living room with my dogs around me and a book in my hand. Fictional trauma I could deal with. This—

All right. This wasn't the first time I'd found a body and Miss Eidt had already fallen apart. She seemed to be melting in the hot sun. I glanced at the sky. When had the sun come out?

"He was shot," I said. "Or stabbed."

She looked at him quickly then looked away. "Was he murdered, do you think? Could he have killed himself?"

"It must have been murder," I said. "But where's the gun or—?"

I didn't see a weapon of any kind...unless he was lying on it.

A sudden thought hovered on the edge of my consciousness. Had the killer fled the scene of his crime? If not, were we in danger?

I didn't see anyone. He could be inside the house, watching, but there was no way to tell. I certainly wasn't going to break in and investigate.

"Look at them," Miss Eidt said with a shiver. "Maybe they're all dead bodies, covered with straw. That's what I thought when I first saw them. This could be a cemetery. They take dead people, roll them in straw—"

She broke off, possibly realizing how insane her theory sounded.

I knew better, but still took a quick look at the gathering of scarecrows. They seemed to avoid my eyes. Silent, unthinking. Harmless?

From the first, however, I had sensed the presence of a watcher. Then there'd been the bridal veil incident and the nightmares... Leonora's and mine.

Miss Eidt was obviously in shock. I hoped I was made of sterner stock.

"They're just scarecrows." I gazed down at the dead man. "We have to call the police. Nine-one-one."

"Do we have to?" she asked. "Couldn't we just leave? Someone is bound to discover it. I mean, him."

"Think, Miss Eidt," I said. "We can't leave him here. Not every crow is afraid of scarecrows. Other birds might find him. Other creatures—"

I fumbled in my purse for my phone.

"But they'll think I killed him," she said.

"Why would anyone think that?"

"I touched the body," she admitted. "I was looking for a pulse. I thought he might be alive at first."

"With all that blood?"

"I wasn't thinking. We have to get out of here, Jennet."

Before my eyes, Miss Eidt was turning into a woman I didn't know. She would never run away from a problem, especially not one that involved breaking the law.

"You didn't even know him," I pointed out. "Why would you kill a stranger? And how?"

I dialed nine-one-one and, again, took her arm. "Let's wait in your car or mine until they get here. Then—"

I considered. She was in shock. After the police came, maybe I should take her to the hospital or even to a nearby diner for a cup of hot tea loaded with sugar.

I swallowed again. Even the thought of sugar-laden hot tea caused my stomach to turn over. But I couldn't be sick. For Miss Eidt's sake. I had to deal with this situation and move on.

"It's like I stepped into one of those Gothic novels," Miss Eidt said. "*A girl stumbles across a body on page two.* But this is really happening."

I made a feeble attempt to lighten the moment. "Look on the bright side. When it's over, you'll have material for a novel of your own."

"There's nothing bright about death, Jennet."

She was right, of course.

"Did you close the library?" I asked.

"I left Debbie in charge. She'll close it. It'll be okay."

"Good," I said, and in light of the unexpected turn the afternoon had taken, I left Crane a voicemail.

The sun grew warmer by the minute. Soon every trace of wet would be burned off the scarecrows. Strange, then, to feel this alien, creeping all-over cold. I felt nauseated again. I looked at the sky, at the road, at the scarecrows, anywhere but at the body.

"The police will be here soon," I said. "We can leave the matter in their capable hands and be on our way."

Twenty

It wasn't so easy. It never is. I should have remembered.

Lieutenant Mac Dalby of the Foxglove Corners Police Department looked at Miss Eidt, his bright blue gaze a steadying force in her fractured world. I was glad he was the one who had answered the call. The tall handsome policeman was an old friend of mine and also of Crane's. He had been present at more than one of my previous adventures, or misadventures, and didn't let me forget it.

Miraculously, he hadn't alluded to them yet.

The ambulance had sped away and taken the body with it. Everyone else had left as well. We were alone: Mac, Miss Eidt, me, and the scarecrows, standing in a crime scene under a burning sky.

I had a brief fancy, a horrible fancy, that the ground under which the dead man had lain had turned to blood.

Mac, who could be gruff and intimidating with me, was gentle with Miss Eidt. I explained that I had driven to the field at her request.

"And..." he turned to Miss Eidt. "You didn't think to call the police right away?"

"Not at first," she said. "I didn't know what to do or if I was in danger."

"Do either of you know the deceased?"

"I never saw him before," I said.

"Miss Eidt?"

"Neither did I."

The man's wallet was missing, leading us to believe he had been robbed, killed, and dumped in this isolated location. He hadn't been wearing a watch. His only accessory was a ring with a huge red stone. You'd think a thief would have taken that...if the motive were robbery.

Mac had made a note of the ring and, undoubtedly reached the same conclusion.

"I can't see anyone go plowing deliberately through a nest of scarecrows," Mac said.

Only Jennet Ferguson and her friends.

He didn't say that, of course, but I suspected he was thinking it.

"All of the scarecrows are for sale," I said. "They're the creations of a lady named Gwendolyn Larkin. She had an ad in the *Banner*."

"I don't see any signs to that effect and the house is vacant," he said.

Miss Eidt fussed with her necklace as if it were choking her. I put my arm around her shoulder.

"Never in my wildest dreams did I expect to find a corpse," she said.

"Tell me again," Mac said. "Why did you come way out here?"

"To look over the scarecrows."

"The scarecrows, yes," he said. "This sure is a weird set-up." He wrote something in his small black notebook. "How did you know they were here? You can't see them from the road."

I answered for her. "I told Miss Eidt about them."

"And I wanted one for the Halloween party at the library," Miss Eidt added.

"The first time I drove by, I noticed the house," I said. "One thing led to another."

"The house. Yes. I wonder who owns it."

That was Mac's question to answer, and I was happy to leave it to him. I didn't want to be a part of a mystery that might include a killer.

Miss Eidt had reached the end of her endurance. "That's all I know, Lieutenant. I found him. I called Jennet. She called you. Do we need to stay? I just want to go home."

Mac nodded. "I'm through here. Don't leave town, Miss Eidt. I may have more questions. That goes for you too, Jennet. How many bodies does this make?"

Ah, there was the condescension. For some perverse reason, I had missed it. I stopped myself from saying, "A hundred and four."

"As if I would go anywhere," Miss Eidt said. "I have a library to run."

"We're not going any place but home," I told him.

As Miss Eidt opened the door to the Camry, she said, "I guess I won't be having a scarecrow at the party."

~ * ~

She's still keeping secrets, I thought as I followed the blue Camry down the road. *But not about the victim. She's told us all she knows, I'm sure.*

Miss Eidt's reaction to the miniature house from the Apple Fair continued to puzzle me. Not that it was necessarily connected to the unknown man who had ended up dead in an isolated field. But it might be.

Possibly, no connection existed. But now, I'd have a reason to quiz Miss Eidt about scarecrows in general. Eventually I'd point the conversation in my own direction, and hope she would be forthcoming. We'd always been good friends, our bond now strengthened by our experience with the murder.

But why, oh why, wouldn't she tell me what prompted her dislike of the miniature house?

Eventually, Crane would have details about the murder. He would also caution me to keep my distance from Scarecrow House.

He wouldn't have to. I had no intention of playing amateur detective. I'd made him a promise once and I was going to keep it.

As I neared Jonquil Lane, my thoughts turned to my life: to dogs, dinner, Crane, and school tomorrow, which was Friday. Our week's goal was due, and I had no idea what to submit.

Now, *that* was traumatic.

~ * ~

Supervised by Candy, Crane locked his gun in its special cabinet. He and I had arrived home at the same time. I started to tell him about the body in the Scarecrow House. As I might have anticipated, he already knew about it. Mac, of course.

Instead of going upstairs for a shower, he poured a glass of lemonade and sat at the oak table, an invitation to confidences. I hoped.

"Did they identify the man?" I asked.

"Not yet. How's Miss Eidt?"

"Shaken, but she'll be all right. If she hadn't decided to see the scarecrows for herself, who knows how long the body might have lain there?"

I shuddered to think of the wild creatures that might have discovered it. Of a flock of vultures undeterred by bunches of straw dressed in expensive clothes. If wildlife had interfered, there wouldn't be much left to identify.

"It's in an out-of-the-way location," Crane said. "I'm sorry you had to get dragged into it."

"I had to help Miss Eidt. In a way, it's my fault she was there. I told her about the scarecrows." A sudden thought surfaced. "They're the property of Gwendolyn Larkin. She'll have to come out of hiding now."

"Why do you think she's hiding?"

"She didn't respond to my voicemails."

"She may be out of town or swamped with orders," he pointed out.

"Or not serious about selling the scarecrows. But then, why bother to place an ad in the paper?"

Why indeed?

I sensed another mystery. This one I intended to pursue. In spite of my negative experience, unlike Miss Eidt, I still wanted to buy a scarecrow.

Twenty-one

The next morning on the way to school, after we'd discussed every aspect of the body in the scarecrow field, Leonora said, "On another subject, did you write your week's goal yet?"

I merged into the southbound lane, happy to see that traffic was light. "Not yet. I still have all day. And no ideas."

"Join the club, but I was thinking. Do you remember how Grimsley was all for team teaching a few years ago?"

I did. He'd subsequently abandoned the idea when it met with half-hearted cooperation from the staff and netted lukewarm results.

"Why don't we present him with a team goal? We can work on it together."

"The only classes we have at the same time are World Literature," I said.

"Then we'll develop our goal for them. Let's talk more about it at lunch."

I liked the idea. Immediately, the chore of creating a goal seemed less daunting. After all, two heads are better than one.

"I thought it could include some kind of giveaway," she said.

"Like?"

"The winner gets a week free of homework."

"Grimsley won't approve of that."

"I guess not. He loves homework. How about a free pizza then? Or concert tickets?"

"That would cost us at least ten dollars. Maybe more."

"That's true.

If Grimsley wanted to move Marston High School up the county ladder, he should be willing to finance our efforts. I, however, didn't want to be the one to suggest this to him.

"How would it work?" I asked.

"We could give each student a number to write on all his papers and have a drawing at the end of the week. Our goal will be...uh... motivation."

"Let's do it," I said. "But it sounds like a bribe."

"Whatever it takes."

At least we'd have something to give Grimsley. It didn't have to be ground-breaking to be acceptable, and he'd be enthusiastic about the idea of team teaching. Suddenly, the day seemed brighter.

"Now we have to decide which selection to teach."

"We'll do that this weekend," I said. "There's a science-fiction story I think they'll like."

~ * ~

At the end of the school day, when all things Marston retreated to the back burner for the weekend, I remembered something I'd only half registered at the time. The sense of somebody watching from the shadows had vanished on that last visit to Scarecrow House when I'd come to Miss Eidt's aid.

Mac himself had pointed out that the house was vacant. Presumably, he'd checked it out. Miss Eidt had only suspected, momentarily, that the killer or killers might have remained on the scene.

On the other hand, could I have been too stunned by the reality of the murder to respond to nuances?

Very unlikely. I was sure I hadn't seen anyone. Nor had Miss Eidt. Besides, where would he or they hide?

I thought about it. On the other side of Mill Road, acres of dark woods, possibly state land, offered privacy for one who didn't worry about snakes, mosquitoes, or other outdoor miseries.

At any rate, I didn't have to worry about unseen watchers as I didn't plan to return to the place. Well, except to pick up my scarecrow, if that were possible, and then Gwendolyn Larkin would be with me.

I placed another call to her, not surprised when it went again to voicemail.

While dinner was in the oven, I scoured the evening *Banner* for news of the murder. A short article on page three contained an appeal to the public. Anyone knowing the victim or having information about the incident was asked to contact the police.

The next day being Saturday, I was free to visit the library. I'd been concerned about Miss Eidt, hoping she'd rebounded from her ordeal. If she was still shaky, a dozen doughnuts from the Hometown Bakery would cheer her. They certainly cheered me.

I found her sitting at her desk staring into space, apparently oblivious of the three teenaged girls, giggling, and turning the paperback carousel with excessive force.

She wore her blue shirtwaist dress again—or did she own more than one?—and a different necklace, long with a double strand of pearls and an ornate glittering clasp. I was sorry to see that she looked unlike herself, pale and detached. Almost haunted. This wasn't good.

She didn't notice me until I set the bakery box in front of her and said good morning.

She blinked and dabbed at her eye with a tissue. "Oh, hello, Jennet. Pastries. How nice."

"How are you holding up?" I asked.

"I'm hanging in there, as the saying goes."

"Is Debbie around?" I asked. "I thought we could have tea and doughnuts in your office."

"What a good idea. Debbie isn't in yet, but I can take a quick break. Sometimes, the library runs itself."

Since when?

As if to disagree with her, the sound of books falling to the floor and a loud accusation broke the silence.

"Look what you did!"

"No, *you* did."

Miss Eidt remained calm but firm. "Be careful, girls. Pick them up."

"Sure, Miss Eidt."

More giggling, another book falling.

She ignored the burgeoning chaos and opened her office door. "Sit down. I'll put the water on, and we'll have tea."

I sat and pushed a stack of library-themed periodicals to the side.

"I was going to call you," Miss Eidt said. "I'm foundering, Jennet. Or is it floundering? I can't think what to do."

"Did something else happen?" I asked

"Read this." She pulled a sheet of paper from her pocket. It consisted of cut-out letters.

"How cliche." I read:

MISS EIDT MURDER WILL OUT CONFESS ANONYMOUS

The words were all different sizes and colors, cut from a magazine or catalogue, even 'Miss Eidt.'

"I didn't kill him," Miss Eidt said. "I swear. You believe me, Mac believes me...I think."

"He does. Where did this come from?"

"It was inside a book left on my desk. A book on knitting, of all things. I didn't see who put it there."

I read the message again, thinking. No one aside from Mac, Crane and I knew Miss Eidt had been anywhere near the crime scene. Someone must have been hiding, watching us. From the woods? Where else?

He could have been driving by. He'd see Miss Eidt, me, and the officers. But not the body that hadn't yet been removed.

Could the note be from the shooter, hoping to deflect attention from himself?

"Tell me what you did yesterday," I said. "Every little detail."

"I parked and walked to the back where you said the scarecrows were. I saw the body right away, but it took me a minute to realize what I was looking at. Like I told Mac, I touched him to see if he was dead. I shouldn't have done that. Then I called you and waited on the porch."

"In all that time you didn't see anyone?"

"I was alone. I thought."

"We didn't see him, but he saw us," I said.

Suddenly I realized the implications of what I had said. If this watcher had seen Miss Eidt, he most likely had also seen me. Just like that, like it or not, I was involved.

"Did you tell Mac about the note?" I asked.

"No. If I do, he'll think I'm guilty."

"No he won't."

Miss Eidt's thoughts were all over the map, as they said.

I folded the paper and gave it back to her. "This is a threat. I can guarantee there'll be another one. Someone, probably the real killer, wants you to take the blame for the murder."

She turned paler, if that were possible. "But why? It makes no sense. None whatsoever."

I had no answer for her. If I were the killer, Miss Eidt was the last person I'd choose to take the fall.

I started as the teakettle whistled, and glanced at the chocolate frosted doughnuts, still in their box. Under ordinary circumstances, they would be irresistible. Neither of us had any interest in them now. But hot tea was another matter. If anything would stop the butterflies from flying around in my stomach, it was a cup of Red Rose.

Miss Eidt poured boiling water over the tea leaves. I swirled my spoon through the fragrant liquid and wondered why my mouth was so dry.

Eventually, we would have to leave Miss Eidt's office. What if the killer was in the library? We had no idea what he, or she, looked like. We couldn't know if we were safe from observation.

"You'd better call Mac now," I said.

"I can't have him come to the library. What would people think?"

"That's the least of your worries. Mac will be discreet. If anyone notices, let them think you're reporting a robbery. Remember, you're the victim here," I added. "You've been threatened."

"And all I wanted was a scarecrow," she said as she reached for her cell phone.

Twenty-two

Debbie was at the front desk when we left Miss Eidt's office and Blackberry lay on an oversized book, as still as a Halloween decoration. The absolute silence in the library struck an eerie note. Usually there was some muted noise...a cough, footsteps, a whisper. Even a book falling accidentally.

The giggling girls had gone on their way, leaving one of the paperbacks on the floor. Inside, like a bookmark, was a Mounds bar wrapper.

Debbie rose, flipping her long yellow braid over her shoulder. "You can have your chair back, Miss Eidt. I'll do the re-shelving."

"Help yourself to the doughnuts," I said.

Seeing the fallen book, Miss Eidt murmured, "Those girls. It's Lucy's *Devilwish*."

I tossed the candy wrapper into the waste basket, returned the book to the carousel, and looked around, wondering again why the library was so quiet. The most comfortable chairs were occupied by people engrossed in their chosen reading material. Others appeared to be looking for the perfect book. A few sat at long tables, writing in notebooks. No one looked like a killer.

But what does a killer look like? Male or female? Young or old? Beady eyed and sinister in appearance, or ordinary like the young woman in beige slacks and a white turtleneck sweater reading the newspaper?

Would the author of the message have stayed close to observe Miss Eidt's reaction to it? I thought he'd leave as soon as he stashed the paper in the nearest book.

"Do you have to go right away, Jennet?" Miss Eidt asked.

I glanced at my watch. "I'll wait till Mac gets here. In the meantime, I'll go browse in the Gothic Nook."

"Good. I'll...I'll wait."

I didn't have the Gothic Nook to myself. Looking like a wraith in a long lace-trimmed gray dress, Edwina Endicott, Foxglove Corner's self-proclaimed ghost catcher, was tossing paperbacks into a basket with abandon, oblivious of Miss Eidt's strictly-enforced limit of four books to a customer at any one time.

Edwina usually haunted the supernatural section where I had encountered her on previous occasions. I imagined a ghost catcher amused herself with fictitious spirits when real ones weren't available.

She held a copy of Henry James' *The Turn of the Screw*. "Good morning, Ms. Greenway," she said. "This is quite the treasure trove, isn't it?"

"It's Mrs. Ferguson," I reminded her. "Call me Jennet."

"Oh, I keep forgetting."

I doubted that. I was pretty sure Edwina remembered my marriage to Foxglove Corners' favorite deputy sheriff.

"This is the best part of the library," I said.

Edwina nodded with enthusiasm. "I could spend the whole day here."

The covered chocolates had vanished. Either Miss Eidt had neglected to fill the candy dishes this morning, or Edwina had emptied them into her basket.

"Why are people so fascinated by ghosts, I wonder," she said.

I shrugged. "The lure of the unknown? A desire to be frightened while remaining safe? Not everybody is a fan of the supernatural, though."

"They're boring down-to-earth people with no imagination. I'm talking about you and me."

Edwina and me. I couldn't help cringing at the unlikely pairing. I didn't like to think I had anything in common with Edwina whom I privately considered a bit unbalanced.

"Visitors from the world beyond have been avoiding Foxglove Corners this fall," Edwina said. "Even Huron Court is just a road. Unless I'm missing something. Have *you* seen any apparitions lately?"

"Well..." Last summer Misty and I had seen the reflection of the phantom collie in the fishpond at Brent's retirement house for dogs. But that was a secret I didn't intend to share with Edwina.

"Not lately," I said. "Maybe they're waiting for Halloween."

"Oh, I *love* Halloween. It looks like Halloween already around here. Miss Eidt must be a frustrated elementary teacher."

I thought of my own bulletin boards at Marston, black and white pictures of American authors framed with colorful paper leaves. In high school, we decorated with a lighter touch.

"Miss Eidt goes all out," I said. "I always look forward to seeing her dollhouse."

"Are you going to the Halloween party?" Edwina asked.

"I wouldn't miss it."

"I had loads of fun last year. Well, I think I'm through here. Happy hunting, Jennet."

In a swish of light gray cotton, she left the Gothic Nook. Automatically, I reached for a chocolate only to remember the dishes were empty. Well, there were still doughnuts in the office.

~ * ~

A full box of pastries was a godsend as Mac was hungry. He accepted a cup of coffee gladly, and, yielding to Miss Eidt's urging, helped himself to a maple-iced doughnut.

With a put-upon sigh, Miss Eidt gave the warning message to him. "I found this in one of our books. It isn't bad enough I have to find a body. Now I'm accused of killing a man I didn't even know."

She sounded less fearful now that she had turned the threat over to Mac.

"Interesting," he said.

"How so?" I asked.

"It looked like the victim was killed elsewhere, and dumped behind the house. Miss Eidt was on the premises for, say, a half hour. Was the killer watching her all that time?"

"Maybe. He might have been looking for a perfect scapegoat," I said.

"He didn't think anyone would notice that one of the scarecrows was a dead person," Miss Eidt said. "That's if anyone would even venture back behind the house."

I voiced a thought I'd had before. "He'd have been smarter to leave the body in the woods. It mightn't have been found for months, if at all. I wonder why he didn't."

We were still talking about the victim, or the dead man. I had been so sure somebody would have identified him by now.

"I can't figure out what's going on here," Mac admitted. "Miss Eidt is the most unlikely killer I've ever met."

"Thank you," Miss Eidt said. "That *is* a compliment, isn't it, Lieutenant?" She topped off his coffee cup. He smiled but didn't answer.

"Now, we have something else to figure out," I said.

"We?" Mac frowned at me.

"You," I said. "The police."

"That's better." He turned to Miss Eidt. "Call me if you get another note like this and watch for anyone acting or looking suspicious."

"That's a tall order. Do you know how many people pass through the library doors every day? Some are regulars. Others..." She sighed again. "I see new faces all the time."

"Do the best you can."

"I will and I'll tell Debbie what's going on. She can be a second pair of eyes."

Mac slipped the message carefully in a small plastic bag. "And I'll hold on to this." He drank the last of the coffee and set the mug on the counter.

"Should I be afraid for my life?" Miss Eidt asked.

Mac didn't answer at once. "We don't know enough about the case, but it's always a good idea to be watchful."

I wished he'd given her a more encouraging answer.

Miss Eidt nodded but her fearful demeanor showed signs of coming back.

She was used to everything running smoothly and quietly in her library, counting on her patrons to share her love of reading. To letting her mind wander on occasion, to letting her attention drift off in one of her books.

I didn't think she'd do well in the role Mac had assigned to her. I was glad she had Debbie.

Twenty-three

Naturally, Miss Eidt didn't want anyone to know she was a suspect in a murder case. This was how she interpreted the note from Anonymous; it was how she thought of herself, in spite of Mac's assurance and support.

I'd pointed out a fact we had both overlooked. "Don't worry about Anonymous going to the police. If he shows his face, Mac will want to know how he came by his information. He'll put himself right at the scene of the crime. And who would be stupid enough to do that?"

This cheered her, but only for a short time.

I wasn't surprised that Brent knew what had happened, nor that he had heard the story from Miss Eidt herself. I learned this on one of his unannounced before-dinner visits.

We sat in the living room drinking coffee as we had many times. Misty was happily settled in Brent's lap, and Sky lay at his feet. Anyone would think they were his dogs.

"We have to do something to help Miss Eidt," Brent said. "She's not dealing with this murder business very well."

"I agree," I said, glad we could discuss the situation openly. "This whole affair has changed her."

I remembered the last time I'd seen her. On the surface, she looked like the same serene and gracious lady who favored pastel suits and classic strands of pearls. But she seemed to have lost interest in the library, which until now had been her reason to get up in the morning.

She didn't even talk about the Halloween party, and her decorating had skidded to a standstill. In my opinion, she'd already done more than enough to dress the library for the season, but she let little things slide. The candy dishes in the Gothic Nook remained empty and she'd stopped bringing in fresh flowers for her desk.

By rights, she should be more at ease. The murdered man had been identified, thanks to a car abandoned on a country road near Maple Creek. It belonged to Jim Morrow, a graduate student at Michigan State. The car had sustained severe damage and the police were unable to locate Morrow.

This discovery led to the identification of the body in the scarecrow field. Morrow was a graduate student with no apparent ties to Scarecrow House. He was last seen at the Brightwater Cider Mill. And how was that for a coincidence?

"What do you think you can do, Fowler?" Crane asked.

"Besides support Miss Eidt? I haven't a clue."

Brent trailed his hand through Misty's thick white ruff and stared into space. He was seldom at a loss for ideas, always ready to charge off to rescue the distressed. But he could hardly fight an unknown killer or challenge a scarecrow.

"One of us should stop by the library every day to make sure Miss Eidt is okay and there are no new developments," I said.

"I've been doing that."

"And?"

"There haven't been any more notes, but Miss Eidt thinks it's only a matter of time before she finds one."

Somewhere in the mix of scarecrows and murder and blackmail, I'd lost track of what might be a crucial part of the mystery: Miss Eidt's possible connection to Scarecrow House before her fateful visit to the field. It centered on the miniature house I'd thought would delight her.

"The little house from the Apple Fair," I said.

"What about it?" Brent asked.

"Miss Eidt didn't like it. She put it away and doesn't talk about it."

Whisked it away out of sight was a more apt description.

"Did you ask her why?" Crane wanted to know.

"Well, no. It's awkward to solicit comments about a gift you give a person. Usually, they're automatic. All Miss Eidt gave me was a bland thank you."

"Maybe she already had one just like it," Brent said.

"No. If that were the case, she would have told me. Besides, the seller said the house was one of a kind."

"That's a mystery then," Crane said.

"It's late in the day, but I can still ask her about it outright. I won't give her a chance to dodge my question."

It was settled then. There was no guarantee she would tell me the truth. Perhaps she would say it wasn't the kind of decoration she wanted to have in the library. With its lifeless dark color and high gables, though, it was perfect for any one of her many Halloween displays.

I could call that to her attention.

Or she might say...What? I couldn't think of another response.

I would ask her and hope she would realize that the time of secrets had passed. How odd it would be if something in Miss Eidt's past tied her to Scarecrow House where she would one day find a body.

~ * ~

Having made up my mind to confront Miss Eidt about the mini-house, I was eager to take action, but other events caused me to postpone my plans. Grimsley called one of his dreaded impromptu staff meetings, resulting in a late arrival home. Star began limping. I took her to the vet the next day after school by which time she was walking normally. We came home with a clean bill of health.

Then, Sue told me that, once again, Velvet had been returned to Rescue. "The new woman claims Velvet isn't happy with them. She sleeps more than a dog her age should and won't play. They want a real dog."

"Poor Velvet," I said. "She *is* a real dog. Why can't she find a home?"

"She hasn't been matched with the right person yet."

"Who is the right person?" I'd asked.

"You," Sue said.

"That was a rhetorical question," I countered.

It kept coming back to me and that was unfair. To be sure, I had coaxed Velvet away from the Fair and was therefore responsible for her. But Sue was the president and adoption coordinator.

"We've been over this, Sue," I said. "I have seven collies. I'd be overwhelmed if I adopted another one."

"Then what will happen to Velvet?" Sue asked.

"Surely I'm not the only person in Foxglove Corners who would give her a good home," I said. "Just keep looking. These other placements weren't meant to be."

Someone out there had to be searching for a tricolor female collie out of puppyhood with Velvet's sweet disposition. That person would let Velvet be herself and wouldn't return her as if she were a garment that didn't flatter the wearer once she looked in a mirror.

"I'm going to take her back to Doctor Foster," Sue said. "If she's sleeping too much, maybe there's a reason."

"That's a good idea, but don't believe everything these people say about her. They just don't want her and she knows it. Sooner or later, you'll find the right owner."

I truly believed that but still I worried about her. Like every dog, Velvet deserved to be in a loving home. I wished it could be with me.

~ * ~

The next person with a claim on my time, or so she assumed, was Tamryn Lynn. As I hadn't heard from her for a while, I thought she'd given up watching for her beloved collie to appear by the lilac tree.

I shuddered at the memory. It was too creepy to contemplate. Whenever I thought of Tamryn's Cara, I felt as if I had stepped into a Stephen King novel.

"Could you come over sometime soon?" she asked.

"Well, I'm pretty busy," I said.

"Just for a brief visit. There's something you have to see."

"Did Cara make another appearance?"

"Better than that."

It was almost six. I remembered the place and time of Cara's previous appearances: the lilac tree around six-thirty. But Tamryn had said 'sometime soon.' It was best to make sure.

"What time should I come?" I asked.

"Around eleven would be perfect. Cara is eager to meet you."

Needless to say, I didn't look forward to that. "How can you be sure she'll be there?"

"Oh, I'm sure," she said. "I found a way to make her stay with me."

Twenty-four

The next morning, I parked in front of Tamryn's house, hoping the visit would be a short one. In my purse, I had a list of errands, any one of which held more appeal than this sojourn into Tamryn's fantasyland.

What had she meant by claiming that she'd found a way to make Cara stay with her?

My question had received a cryptic reply. "You'll see tomorrow."

I therefore drew my own conclusion. What Tamryn claimed was impossible, unless she was referring to a pawprint cast in plaster or a special picture. Or perhaps a video she could watch whenever she so desired? None of that was real.

Did I want to know?

At the moment, I was only mildly curious, content to hear the answer in passing at some future time. Now that I was here, however...

I grabbed my purse and locked the car. Breathing in crisp, cool air fragrant with a hint of burning leaves, I walked to the house.

It had the disconsolate appearance of one long abandoned. Drapes closed tightly over the picture window, and layers of crimson leaves lay heavily on the walkway, on the porch, and right up to the garage built to imitate the house's lines and colors. Nobody had walked this way or driven a car out to the street in a while. Didn't that suggest that Tamryn was inside?

You'd think so, but it looked as if she wasn't home.

That couldn't be. Only last night she had set the time. Eleven o'clock. Saturday. *This* Saturday.

I crunched my way through the leaves and rang the doorbell, listening to its jarring ring. Idly, I studied the wreath on the door, a grapevine circlet adorned with small faux pumpkins.

Seconds ticked by. No footsteps approached; no one opened the door. I even listened for the sound of a dog barking an alert. Finally, I glanced at my watch. Five minutes to eleven. I rang the bell again and waited.

Darn. Had Tamryn done it again? Tricked me into coming to her house for no discernible purpose?

One more time...

I pressed on the doorbell again hard and kept my finger on it.

You're dealing with a nutcase, I told myself. *She's not here. Maybe she planned it this way for some twisted reason.*

Why did I persist in thinking of Tamryn as an ordinary person? More to the point, how had I gotten mixed up in her bizarre affairs in the first place?

To bring a dead dog back to life by scattering its ashes. Honestly.

Tamryn needed help to deal with her grief and I wasn't qualified to provide it. Which was what I had told Sue Appleton in the beginning.

I kicked at a drift of maple leaves, watched them sail off the porch to join their fellows on the ground and felt marginally better. I was through being dragged into whatever game Tamryn was playing.

Without a backward glance, I returned to the car and headed for the nearest road that would take me to the Corners. I hoped I'd have better luck with Miss Eidt.

~ * ~

I welcomed the sameness that greeted me at the library. On the porch, Blackberry reclining in the wicker rocker, fixing me with her inscrutable green stare. Miss Eidt's wreath with its wood-cut figures inspired by vintage Halloween cards. Leaves raked into the flower beds, no doubt by Debbie who welcomed an occasional outdoor chore.

I felt as if I were coming to my second home.

A vase filled with red roses on Miss Eidt's desk caught my eye as soon as I stepped inside. What a departure from the grocery store bouquets she usually bought. I came closer, enough so that their rich fragrance rolled over me.

Exquisite! Did this mean Miss Eidt was emerging from her fear-induced malaise?

She came up behind me. "Aren't they beautiful?"

"Absolute perfection."

"Brent brought them this morning. You just missed him." She twisted her long rope of pearls, and let it fall back on the ruffled bodice of her beige dress. "They make me happy every time I look at them."

Which was Brent's intention, of course.

"Brent is always thinking of others," I said.

He was one step ahead of me. I wished I'd thought to stop at the Hometown Bakery. Pastries would pave the way for the heart-to-heart talk I hoped we would have.

"He brought me a dozen doughnuts, too, and it isn't even my birthday."

Miss Eidt looked more like herself, almost happy, and didn't give the impression that she was waiting for something terrible to happen.

"Has everything been peaceful in the library?" I asked.

"Pretty much, with one exception. This morning I had a run-in with Natty Smith."

"Who's he?"

"A man who lives to break rules. You know I don't allow eating or drinking in the library." She glanced at the doughnuts. "Except in my office, naturally. This is my private area."

I nodded.

"He brought in an entire carry-out breakfast: French toast, bacon, hash browns, even coffee. Debbie saw him and told me."

"What happened then?"

"This was his third offense. I told him to leave the library. He swore and threw his plate at me."

"Incredible. Even my worst students haven't sunk that low."

"I told him not to return. Luckily, I had a clean dress in the closet. At least I didn't get another anonymous message. Do you think it was all a bluff?"

"Probably not, but we'll have to wait and see."

What I thought was that Anonymous was merely biding his time. I said, "Do you have a few minutes for us to talk?"

"Always. I'm so glad you stopped by today."

"For any special reason?"

"I want to keep my friends close around me. We'll go to my office. Debbie's around here somewhere. She'll take care of the library."

In her office, Miss Eidt filled the teakettle and put it on the burner. She opened the bakery box. "Just look. All chocolate frosted. My favorite."

There were an even dozen. It was as if Miss Eidt had been waiting for me to share them with her.

"And they're still warm," she added.

I saw no point in waiting to introduce the subject subtly. "I have to ask you something, Miss Eidt. It's important."

She set two mugs and paper plates on the table. "That sounds serious. Did something else happen?"

"In a way. Do you remember the little wood-carved house I brought you from the Apple Fair?"

She looked down and moved the mugs to the other side of the plates, then reached for a stack of paper napkins. "Of course I do. It was only a few weeks ago."

"I thought it would fit right in with the Gothic Nook décor, especially for Halloween."

"It was a thoughtful gift. I couldn't go to the Apple Fair this year, so it was nice to have a souvenir."

Nice. Was ever a word less flattering?

"I got the impression you didn't like it," I said.

She paused, choosing her doughnut with great care. "Surely I didn't say that?"

"No, but actions speak louder than words. Where is it now?"

She paused, glancing at the cupboard. "It's around. Someplace."

"You hate it or it makes you uneasy. I wonder why."

The teakettle whistled, giving Miss Eidt an opportunity to delay answering me. After arranging six doughnuts on a plate, she said, "You're too perceptive, Jennet."

"Well, you were pretty obvious."

She cut her doughnut into neat halves. "All right, there is something. The house reminds me of an unhappy time in my past. I don't like to think about it and I never talk about it."

How to get around that? "It might be relevant to what's going on now."

"Oh, I don't think so."

"Does it have anything to do with Scarecrow House?" I asked.

She sighed. "I see you won't let this go."

"I want to help. You have to admit the carving is an exact replica of that old house."

"It could be."

"And if it is?"

She busied herself brewing our tea, pouring boiling water over measures of loose Red Rose, adding spoons to the table. "Then I don't know what's going on," she said.

Twenty-five

I swirled my spoon through the tea, watching the leaves sink to the bottom of the cup. I wasn't sure what Miss Eidt had meant by that last remark.

"Do you mean with the murder?" I asked.

"That, too, but I'm thinking about the little house. When I saw it, it seemed like it was a message to me."

"What kind of message"

"I'm not sure. Let me restate that. It was like an unwelcome reminder from the past. I never expected to see that house again, but there it was, in miniature, under all that wrapping. And it came from you. Tell me, how did you come to buy it?"

"I noticed it when I was shopping for a fall wreath," I said. "Right away, I thought of you and the Gothic Nook, like I said. I never found my wreath."

She nodded. "I couldn't believe that such a thing existed. A mirror image of that house."

"I was told it was one of a kind."

"Yes, and so was that house. My question is who could have made it? And why?"

"I have no idea. The artist didn't sign it. As to why...who knows? It's an attractive little decoration. Perhaps that's all there is to it."

"Maybe I'm imagining things," she said.

She didn't sound convinced. And it seemed as if she wasn't going to tell me any more about that mysterious time in her past without prompting.

I said, "If Scarecrow House has unhappy associations for you, why did you go there?"

"To see the scarecrows. That's all I could think about at the time. In retrospect, it was a mistake. But what happened was so long ago..."

She trailed off, concentrated on eating her doughnut and washed it down with a long sip of tea.

"What *did* happen?" I asked. "Can you tell me?"

"It has absolutely no bearing on the murder," she assured me. "It was entirely personal."

"Could you let me be the judge of that?"

"Well...I may tell you sometime, Jennet. But not now. Not today."

I had to be content with that as I had no desire to badger Miss Eidt and cause her more anxiety. Coincidences do exist, and quite likely, I had stumbled across one.

"Have another doughnut," Miss Eidt said. "I'll pour us some more tea. Amazing how it cools off so quickly."

"Are you going to keep the little house out of sight?" I asked.

"I guess I can put it someplace in the Gothic Nook—and forget about it. Will that make you happy?"

"Only if you want to," I said.

"I'll do it," she said. "It's a house of death, after all."

~ * ~

All the way home, I pondered Miss Eidt's last comment. A house of death.

She might be referring to the murder that had taken place on the premises or an incident in the past she guarded so zealously. How could I tell? It was clear, though, that she was referring to the big house rather than the miniature.

As I drove down the lonely country roads, I reviewed what I knew about Miss Eidt. There wasn't much, but that was understandable. My friends and I rarely talked about our pasts, preferring to dwell in the present, which had its own joys, and traumas, and triumphs.

I knew that Miss Eidt, a native of Foxglove Corners, had donated her family home to the town to use as a library. Many of the books, the older ones, came from her private stores. She had then purchased a smaller, more easily maintained house not too far away.

I wondered what had prompted her decision to surrender that spacious white Victorian sitting so proudly on its half-acre of landscaped grounds. Of course, she was there almost every day, with the help of Debbie keeping the library open long hours to serve the town's readers. She had, in effect, two homes.

And that was all?

No. I remembered the secret, haunted room of whose existence even she hadn't been aware. It was closed up now, never used, and almost forgotten.

All right. That was all.

Miss Eidt's years as a young woman were a mystery to me. Where she was educated, whether she had ever been married or had lived elsewhere in Michigan, or another state...

I saw her as the perennial librarian dressed in pastel suits with a collection of pearl necklaces, a sweet, helpful friend, the caretaker of Foxglove Corner's past and a lover of baked goods.

Now I learned she had lived through an unhappy time, so unhappy that years later she didn't want to talk about it, and it involved Scarecrow House, the real one, and possibly events that culminated in a murder.

I was suddenly curious to know all about Miss Eidt, about the years she never mentioned. How I could manage that was another mystery. I cared too much for her to harass her when she had made it clear she wanted to keep her secret, and certainly, I wasn't going to try to find out in any other way.

Where did that leave me? Leave us, I should say. Leave the mystery of the murder at Scarecrow House?

In limbo, I decided, but I had a suspicion that enlightenment lay just ahead…along with some other event I might or might not welcome.

~ * ~

Back home, I took care of the collies, then walked Misty, Star, and Gemmy to Sue Appleton's horse ranch. I was still annoyed that Tamryn hadn't kept our appointment and intended to officially withdraw my offer to help her recover from the loss of her collie.

But wait! Had I offered to help or was I badgered? Sue was used to getting her own way. She had to be with an endless stream of rescues to pick up and place, and a small number of League members who always had other things to do.

Sue was outside enjoying the beautiful fall day with all of her collies and her horses in the background. The breeze which had grown stronger blew her long strawberry blonde hair in her face. It whipped the dogs' coats into motion as they ran aimlessly around the barn and sent leaves whirling through the air.

Velvet detached herself from the pack and ran up to me, wagging her tail and nudging my knee with her nose. Just as if she were my dog greeting me after a long absence.

"How've you been, Velvet girl?" I asked.

Sue answered for her. "She's like any other of my dogs. I don't know what that woman who gave her back to me was talking about."

"I told you. She just didn't want her. I can't imagine why."

I gave Velvet more than her fair share of patting. She appeared to revel in it, making me feel a bit guilty. Did she greet every visitor this way?

"She remembers you," Sue said.

"She should. The Apple Fair wasn't that long ago."

Rudely, Scarlet nudged her out of the way, wanting attention for herself.

We let the dogs finish greeting one another, then sat on the porch with them grouped around us, as it was still warm enough to do so and the fair weather wouldn't last much longer. It was our duty to savor every precious day. I told Sue about Tamryn.

"Well, she's unreliable," Sue said. "I hope she doesn't persist in trying to join the Rescue League again."

"You'll just have to make it clear to her."

"I did, in a letter. Not face to face. The integrity of the League and the welfare of our dogs come before anyone's hurt feelings. If Tamryn objects, she can always change her ways." Sue leaned forward in her chair. "You didn't really expect to see Cara, did you, Jennet?"

"I didn't know what to expect. Tamryn said she'd found a way to make Cara stay with her. She refused to explain."

"You know that's impossible."

"Yes. I should have made an excuse."

"You'll know the next time."

"There won't be a next time," I said.

Twenty-six

Since I obviously wasn't going to learn more about the story behind the Scarecrow House from Miss Eidt, I decided to drive out to the cider mill for more apples. Then I'd stop at the house on the way, that being the more important destination.

I didn't expect to find anything significant, but you never can tell. I felt relatively safe visiting the former crime scene. Surely the killer wasn't lurking in the woods spying on the scarecrow field on the off chance that someone would wander by. Even if he were, what business would he have with me?

If anyone challenged me, I'd say I just stopped to look at the scarecrows.

On the other hand, why court trouble? I'd take one of the collies with me. Misty. Because of her sixth sense, she had been invaluable to me in the past.

After taking steaks out to defrost for dinner, and enjoying a quiet Sunday walk with three collies, I led Misty out to the car and set a course for Mill Road.

Silhouetted against a dark, cloud-filled sky that threatened rain, Scarecrow House held fast to its singular melancholy air. I wondered if it had looked the same when it had played a part in Miss Eidt's past.

What a difference a lighter shade of paint would make, beige perhaps with brown shutters and trim, along with fresh landscaping and no sinister scarecrow peering around the corner.

I could almost see a younger Miss Eidt standing in front of the porch as if posing for a picture. She wore a gray skirt and white sweater with a pearl necklace. Her hair was long and blonde rather than silvery gray. In my vague imaginings, a tall figure stood behind her, obscured by shadows. She didn't appear to be aware of him.

Darn! I wish I knew the whole story.

I attached Misty's collar to her leash and led her out of the car. The loud rustle of feet mashing down leaves sounded ominous in the country silence. A gust of wind whipped dried leaves and other debris in my face. Impatiently, I brushed them away.

Misty gave a little yelp of excitement at the prospect of exploring a new place. As she spied the scarecrows, her tail wagged enthusiastically. She lunged for Imogen, the closest one, who tottered on her pole at the assault. I pulled back on the leash and leaned against the wall of the house, counting scarecrows.

They still numbered eleven, and their outfits retained the crisp look of new clothing in spite of the numerous storms and winds they had withstood.

And I still wanted one.

But...something nagged at me, some half-remembered difference. I took another look and saw it at once. One scarecrow sported a long black cloak whose white underside flapped in the wind.

Dracula.

As I came closer, Misty lunged again, took an edge of the cloak in her mouth, and pulled.

"Misty, no!"

I freed the material from her death grip and drew her to my side.

Hadn't a cloak covered the body Miss Eidt had found? I thought so, in which case, this had to be another one, the original having been removed for evidence. It suggested that Gwendolyn Larkin, the scarecrow's maker, had visited the field recently, bringing with her a duplicate cloak.

Then Gwendolyn knew about the murder. The police must have caught up with her. Why hadn't she returned my call?

Call again, I thought. I wanted my scarecrow while the season was still autumn.

Keeping a tight rein on Misty, I examined the area carefully but didn't see anything out of place. Nor were there any clues on the ground. But then, if there had been, Mac would have scooped them up.

"There's nothing to find here," I informed Misty. "We might as well go on to the cider mill before it rains."

Her ears shot up. I didn't realize she recognized the words 'cider mill,' although she knew what doughnuts were. Could she have made the connection?

Clever collie!

She started as thunder rolled across the sky. Dracula's cape flapped higher in the wind. I glanced up at the darkening clouds, and for a second saw a fleeting movement behind one of the windows on the second floor of the house...where no movement should be.

Somebody was there watching us. In a heartbeat, the person or thing vanished.

A warm raindrop landed on my arm, the first of a hardy splattering.

Hurry! I told myself. *Get in the car!*

Instead, another Jennet, the impossibly impulsive one, moved toward the back porch, half dragged by seventy pounds of exuberant collie.

A door led into the house. Oddly, it was ajar. The invitation was irresistible.

Knowing this was quite possibly the most idiotic thing I'd ever done, I rapped on the door.

"Hello? Is anybody there?"

My voice echoed in the hollow halls. If someone was inside the house, I had an excuse ready: I'd like to buy one of the scarecrows.

Of course, there was no answer.

To my credit, I hesitated on the threshold for a moment, reflecting on what I was about to do. It couldn't be called breaking and entering if the door was open. And what if someone inside was in need of help with no way to summon it?

I had a single sensible thought. What if a killer waited upstairs eager to strike?

That wasn't likely. Besides, I had Misty for protection, and I'd been wanting to explore the house from the moment I realized it was vacant.

Stepping down hard in the hope of announcing my presence, I walked into a current of stale, unwholesome air. Misty, in this instance smarter than her mistress, put on her brakes, but I tugged on the leash gently and she moved with me.

It was stuffy and hard to breathe. As if in agreement, Misty sneezed twice.

The porch led into what was possibly a bedroom. Beyond lay a hall steeped in darkness. The room was empty, as I'd assumed was the case in the entire house.

But someone was there. Upstairs.

"Hello," I said again.

Misty pointed her nose toward the hall. *Let's go!*

"I'm coming up," I said, but hesitated in the living room.

The darkness that had accompanied the storm made me uneasy. I had a miniature flashlight in my glove compartment and an App on my phone. Automatically, I reached into my pocket. It was empty except for a tissue. With a sinking heart, I realized that in my haste to check out the scarecrow field, I'd left my phone in my purse, and my purse in the car.

Now what?

Maybe I wasn't going upstairs after all.

Rain pounded on the old windows. They seemed to shriek in protest but held on in spite of the onslaught.

Go out through the front door, I thought. *The car's in the driveway. You'll only get a little wet.*

"Misty, come!"

We were halfway to the door when a low drawn-out moan froze me in place. Misty started barking. It seemed as if she would never stop.

For the first time that day, I didn't know what to do.

Twenty-seven

It didn't take long for me to decide, not even half a second. I couldn't run in the opposite direction if someone was in trouble. That moan had sounded like a cry for help.

As I led Misty to the staircase, I noticed a scattering of leaves on the hardwood floor, one more indication that someone was inside the house.

Again, Misty balked at ascending a strange staircase, but I would never leave her behind. She was my responsibility and my protector. Most importantly, I loved her.

"Come!" I used my rare no-nonsense tone, holding tightly to her leash, and she moved, albeit reluctantly.

More leaves lay strewn on the steps. The staircase was narrower than the one we were used to at home. On my left, the wallpaper, a faded ivory-light green color sprinkled with bunches of violets, was peeling in places. Apparently no one had given this house any care in a long time.

"Hold on," I called out. "We're on our way."

I expected to hear some response. 'Oh, thank heavens,' perhaps, or 'I need help' or even another moan, but the only sounds besides the pounding rain were our footfalls, Misty's and mine.

At times, silence is menacing. It can be deadly. Jabs of fear spiraled through me as I wasn't totally foolhardy. At least, I didn't think so.

Pushing aside the thought that the person who moaned had already expired, I stood at the top of the stairs, listened, and waited. Misty uttered a plaintive whine, all her earlier exuberance at exploring a new place gone.

Now that I'd reached my destination, I had a brief urge to retrace my steps and run out into the rain to the safety of my car.

A coward's thought, but also justifiable. A half-heard threat trembled in the air.

I took a few hesitant steps and climbed the rest of the way to the second story, stopping when I reached the top to survey the scene that lay before me.

The hall was dark and forbidding. Half of the doors were closed and half ajar as the door to the porch had been. The person who had moaned must be behind one of them, but all was quiet except for the rain.

Still I called, "Where are you?"

No answer. Misty whined and turned around, pointing in the direction of the stairs. She didn't want to venture any further into unknown territory. Neither did I, but I'd come this far...

I pushed open the first door on my right and beheld a small, empty room. Cobwebs decorated the corners and woodwork around the windows and they hung in long wispy ropes from the old-fashioned light fixture. I shuddered at the thought of unseen spiders and moved down the hall, opening doors, seeing more of the same.

My nerves were wound so tightly, I feared they'd snap at the slightest wrong move, but at this point, I had no choice but to go on.

All of the rooms on the left side were empty as was the bathroom at the end of the hall. In there, the fixtures were a washed-out shade of pale blue, and the tiles on the floor and halfway up the walls were gray-and-white, the gray repeated in swatches of mold.

I turned on the faucet and watched a stream of rust-colored water flow into the wash basin.

Someone must be in the house besides me—unless what I'd heard was the house settling. In the middle of the day? In a rainstorm? Not very likely. A house settling didn't sound like a person moaning.

"Is anyone here?" I asked again. "I'll help you."

A lightning bolt split the sky. It might well have split the roof, given the jolt I felt. For a heartbeat, the hall burst into light, then fell back to dimness.

I opened the next door. This room, too, was empty and seemingly innocuous, but menace thickened the air. At my side, Misty came to a stop, her body as rigid as a statue carved in stone.

What in the name of everything that is holy was I doing?

Behind you! Turn around!

As the thought took shape, a rustling sound insinuated itself into the silence. A rustle, a breath, a footstep...

Misty growled; a low angry, warning sound I'd never heard her make.

A great weight crashed down on the top of my head. Consciousness left my body.

~ * ~

The lightning struck again. It split my head open. I'm going to die...

I opened my eyes to a sickening sensation of pain and nausea and quickly closed them again. I touched the top of my head lightly, half expecting to see blood when I withdrew it. There was no blood, only pain.

Dear God, my worst headache had never been so severe.

I tried to lift my head, but the pain forced it back down to the hardwood floor. Nausea overcame me. I felt as if I were going to lose my muffin-and-tea-breakfast.

No. Breathe. Wait. Let it pass.

Something had hit me. No, someone.

Who? Who could have moved so soundlessly that I hadn't been aware of an alien presence until it was too late? Who could have crept up on me under Misty's radar?

Only one answer came to mind. The person who had moaned. He had hidden himself well. Somewhere. Beyond one of the doors I hadn't opened?

That moan hadn't been real. It had been a lure. And I'd fallen for it.

Yes, fallen. I've fallen and I can't get up.

I placed my other hand on the gritty floor and tried to lever myself up, which should have been easy but wasn't.

My other hand?

Suddenly the full horror of what had happened broke over me. Where was—

Misty?

She wasn't at my side! Her leash wasn't in my hand!

"Misty!"

My voice sounded weak, its echo weaker still. She wouldn't be able to hear me. I called her name once again, forcing my voice into a semblance of a feeble shout.

"Misty! Come!"

Whoever struck me that devastating blow might have done worse to my dog. What had possessed me to bring her to this place of danger?

Half crawling, I forced my body across the floor to the door. Reaching my destination, I leaned against the wall.

Think! You have to get out of this room. Out of this accursed house.

I had to find Misty. If I could only stand. If I could move my head.

No ifs. I had to *make* myself move. No one else would help me. But the throbbing in my head only grew worse.

I needed to take something for it. I always carried pain pills in my purse in case a headache came on at school.

Another horrible thought took form. My car! Was the Focus still parked outside the house? I'd left it unlocked, and tossed the keys on top of my purse, an invitation to a thief to drive it away. I had to get up to see if I did indeed have a way to escape Scarecrow House.

Do it then!

It wasn't so easy. I took a few steps, then a few more, but I was unsteady on my feet. Could I walk all the way down the stairs and across the living room? The first slight movement pushed the throbbing on top of my head so high I could barely stand it. I had never needed that pain medication more.

Dear God...Misty. Help me.

Tears burned in my eyes, fell freely down my face. I remembered the tissue in my pocket but didn't bother with it.

My pestiferous inner voice chose that moment, when I was at my most vulnerable, to make herself heard: 'Serves you right, Jennet. You couldn't leave well enough alone. You had to let curiosity overcome your good sense.'

All right. Guilty as charged. Now I had to act. I had to find Misty. I needed to feel her leash firmly grasped in my hand, needed to feel my precious collie pressing against my body. The rest would be easy.

Finally I made it to the door. I held on to the doorknob as I stepped cautiously out into the hall, momentarily, cheered by a fantasy.

My dog would be there lying in the hall, guilty of selective hearing as many collies are at one time or another. She'd rise slowly, stretch, come toward me.

She wasn't there.

What I saw instead threw my heart into an unhealthy racing pattern. Long strands of straw lay mixed with the trail of leaves in the hallway.

Twenty-eight

My assailant was a scarecrow!

The idea was so ludicrous that I rejected it out of hand. Just because I saw a few strands of straw in the hall. Just because my last memory had been of a rustle. Just because...

Scarecrows weren't alive. They were figures fashioned of coarse material and straw. They had features drawn on with paint and wore clothing purchased especially for them if they were the special denizens of Scarecrow House.

They didn't have voices to moan, they didn't walk, and certainly they were incapable of launching an attack on a human.

It was a fellow human who had come up behind me and dealt that horrible blow.

However, once the idea of a scarecrow attacker dropped into my mind, it refused to be dislodged. After all, this was Foxglove Corners, Home of the Strange, where anything was possible.

Okay. Believe what you will. A scarecrow came to life and hit you on the head. It's gone now. You'd better get out of here before it comes back.

Wishing I had a cane, I tottered to the head of the staircase. The stairs seemed to swim before my eyes, twisting and turning, disappearing in a thin white fog that began to fill the first floor. Tendrils drifted up the stairs to meet me.

It's only because of the pain in my head, I told myself. *Pain distorting reality.*

Could I make my way down the stairs to the first floor? All the way down?

Hold on to the railing. Don't let go and you won't fall.

I took the first step. All right. Now the next.

A sudden pounding fractured the silence. It was outside my head. Downstairs. Someone was pounding on the front door.

Scarecrows can't knock on a door.

It could only be a person, someone, I hoped, who would help me.

"Jennet! Are you in there? Open the door!"

Oh my God. That was Brent's voice, however unlikely it seemed. Deliverance was at hand, at the bottom of the staircase, beyond the white fog.

"I'm inside," I called out. "I'm...hurt."

He'd never be able to hear that.

I tried again. "I'm here. In the house."

The pounding continued. I made a tremendous effort to move forward and at last reached the bottom of the staircase. The floor. *Terra firma.* The fog seemed to dissipate as I stumbled toward the door and pulled it open. And there on the other side stood Brent, his dark red hair gleaming with raindrops, his fist poised for another assault on the door.

A wildly excited Misty danced around him, crying shrilly. She leaped at me. I fell back against the door. Brent pulled me forward while Misty sniffed at my skirt.

"My little girl!" I cried. "Oh, thank God. Thank you."

Brent held a large, jagged piece of material, bright florals on a black background. A long line of red stained its edge. He glanced at the stain and shoved it into his pocket.

"What the hell happened to you?"

"It's a long story." Skipping over the beginning, over the details, I told him the important part. "Someone came up behind mem and hit me hard enough to—"

I touched the top of my head, felt a warm swelling and winced as waves of pain surged around me.

"Who did this to you?"

Without thinking how ridiculous it sounded, I said, "One of the scarecrows."

He stared at me, incredulous. "How hard did he hit you?"

"Hard enough. Can you help me to my car?"

He took hold of my hand. "Not so fast. How did you get in the house in the first place? The doors were locked."

"The one in back was open."

I wasn't in any condition to answer questions, but he persisted. "And you just went inside? What were you thinking?"

I tossed him a question of my own. "How did you know I was here?"

"Your car," he said. "I was coming back from the cider mill and saw it. Then I saw Misty running around the house like a wild thing. But I didn't see you. I knew you were in there. I was seconds away from breaking the door down."

Someone must have closed the porch door, effectively locking Misty outside. But before that happened, she must have gone after him. Had she ripped the floral material from his body as he tried to escape her?

Brent held on to me as I walked shakily to the car, Misty leaping and yelping in front of me. I leaned against the Focus' damp door, not caring that my long denim skirt was getting wet.

"Whatever brought you here, I'm glad to see you."

"Coincidence. I wanted to give the men at the barn a treat."

"Did you buy cider?" I asked.

"I loaded up on it. I have doughnuts too."

"I'd like a drink," I said. "I have to take some pills."

He shook his head. "That's a bad idea. You need to get that head checked out first."

He took firm hold of my hand and led me to his vintage Plymouth.

"You mean at Emergency? I don't want to do that. I just want to go home and go to bed. What time is it?" I added. "I don't have my watch."

"Just after two. The sheriff will have my head if I let you drive."

I balked at letting control slip out of my hands. Surely I could drive if I took it slowly on the little-traveled country roads.

"I'm not going to leave my car here," I said.

"It'll be all right for a while. I'll take you to the hospital then take Misty home and send one of the men to come back for your car.'

The terrible pounding convinced me that Brent was right. Besides, arguing with him took more energy than I had at present.

He opened the door and I sank back against the seat. Afraid she was going to be left behind, Misty yipped and waited for him to open the back door. She settled herself in the back seat and Brent reached into his pocket for his keys. I remembered the piece of material.

"Where did you get that rag or whatever it is?"

"I took it from Misty. She had it in her mouth."

"Is that blood on it?"

He pulled it out of his pocket and shook it out. "Looks like it."

"One of the scarecrows had a shirt like that."

"Keep talking about scarecrows and I'll know you have a concussion," Brent said.

"I was talking about a shirt or whatever it is. Was. Could I have that drink now?"

"Sure thing."

He walked around to the trunk and returned with a gallon of cider and an empty thermos. "Here you go. It might smell like coffee." He twisted the top off the container in one quick motion.

I didn't care what it smelled like. Just so it was liquid. I took a long swallow. I hadn't realized my throat was so dry.

Soon he had the Plymouth going. I sighed as I remembered my original plan. Apples from the cider mill. Doughnuts. Caramel apples and, maybe, fudge. You never know how a day that begins with high hopes will end.

"You could have died in that old house and who would have known?" Brent sounded suspiciously like Crane. He was right, though. Strange that possibility hadn't occurred to me until then.

That blow on the head could have been wielded with enough force to kill and what a stupid way that would have been to die. And my Misty. She would have been stranded in unfamiliar territory, miles from home. She might have been hit by a car.

"That's true, but I didn't realize anyone else was in the house until I heard a moan. I thought I was helping somebody."

"There's a moral in that story," he said, again sounding like my dictatorial deputy sheriff husband.

I didn't want to pursue morals at the moment.

"The sheriff isn't going to be happy," Brent added.

I sighed again. That was an understatement if ever I heard one.

"I'll deal with him later," I said.

Twenty-nine

My stay in Emergency swallowed up the rest of the afternoon. Brent took care of my car and Misty, so all I had to do was lie on a narrow bed and watch the hands of the clock slowly move forward. He also notified Crane, who hurried to my side and, thankfully kept any thoughts of recrimination he might have to himself.

My reward was a clean bill of health and a trip home instead of admission to the hospital, which I feared might happen. All was well, but it could have been so much worse.

The collies knew something was wrong with me but weren't sure what to do about it. I didn't reach for the Lassie tin, didn't let them out, and my hand, still shaky, rested on only the nearest soft heads. The lucky dogs were Candy and Gemmy.

Crane told them to go lie down.

I eyed the steaks with disinterest. Crane saw them, too.

"I'll put them back and get us a pizza for dinner," he said. "You need to rest."

"That'll work." I sank into another seat, this one the oak chair. It had never seemed harder.

I touched the top of my head again. I couldn't seem to keep my hand away from it, as if that would make the pain go away. It would more likely have the opposite effect.

Crane opened the side door and the dogs gathered around him with wagging tails. Except for Misty. She was practically glued to my side.

Closing my eyes, I reviewed the day. What could I have done differently? For one, ignore the lure of the open porch door. I had walked blithely into enemy territory and paid the price for my blunder. I should have realized that if the door was open, there was a good chance someone would be inside.

I could also have just driven by the scarecrow field and gone directly to the cider mill. If only I could live the day over and this time really think about my choices.

The collies burst through the door, Candy in the lead, Sky and Raven bringing up the rear. Halley rushed to my side, pushing Misty aside.

"Collies taken care of," Crane announced. He refilled their water bowls and set them on the floor with aplomb.

He spilled the contents of the Lassie tin on the floor, and we watched the dogs pounce on them.

"I'm so lucky to have you," I told him.

"You better believe it."

He filled the teakettle, found a mug, and sprinkled a large measure of Red Rose in it. "This may help."

"It will. Thank you."

While I waited for the water to come to a boil, my thoughts drifted back to my trauma in Scarecrow House. "If only I'd seen who struck me."

"Someone who was inside Scarecrow House, whether he had a right to be there or not."

Like me, I thought.

"We'll track him down. Mac already has the investigation going."

"Well...I've been thinking, or rather trying to. If he's the homeowner, he might say he was defending his property from an intruder."

"He just left you there to die. My guess is he was an intruder himself."

"He must have been surprised to see Misty."

I wished I knew what had transpired while I was unconscious. I imagined Misty had set upon my attacker, ultimately tearing a piece of his clothing. Somehow he must have gotten her out of the house. Then would he have left himself? There were too many holes in the story for me to make sense of it.

Unbidden, a thought came to me. Could he have been in the house all along, tending to his wound while I struggled back to consciousness? Was he still there?

Crane let his hand fall on Misty's head. "Good Misty."

She had been protecting me as a good dog should, but I could almost hear an accusation bouncing back at us in a hostile voice. "That vicious dog bit me. She needs to be put down."

I remembered the blood on the floral rag. My assailant's blood.

What was wrong with me? I never used to be so fearful. If he dared to accuse Misty, he'd have to answer for his attack on me.

"Maybe they can ID the jerk if his fingerprints are on that cloth Misty had in her mouth," I said.

"If they're on file."

The teakettle whistled. Crane poured boiling water in the mug, not without splashing some of it on the table. I was the family tea maker.

"I'll get us that pizza," he said. "You take care of Jennet, Misty."

"I'll be all right," I said.

He rested his hand heavily on my shoulder. "You sure know how to liven up a boring day."

~ * ~

When he came back with the pizza, Crane also had an apple pie from Clovers with Annica's best wishes for a quick recovery.

"I can't lose you, Jennet," he added, "but sometimes I think that's going to happen. You've been in the line of fire so many times. More than I have and that's saying something."

I nodded. "Even on a simple errand to buy cider and doughnuts."

I didn't want to lose him either, or the wonderful life we'd built together.

He said, "Who knew that scarecrow business would turn out to be so dangerous?"

Well, I did, but I thought it prudent not to say anything. From the beginning, there was something odd about all those scarecrows huddled together behind the house. I hadn't forgotten Leonora's reaction or the body covered with Dracula's cape. To that, add the miniature house and Miss Eidt's mystery, to say nothing of Gwendolyn Larkin's long silence.

Yes, danger was a given, but I couldn't know that it would come in the form of a blow on the head.

"Do you still want a scarecrow for the house?" Crane asked as he paused at the bottom of the stairs.

"No. I mean, yes. Maybe."

I'd long since discarded the idea that my attacker was a scarecrow. Anyone could track straw and leaves into a house.

"How about if I bring up the old one? You can put other decorations on it, and it'll be like new."

"That'll work," I said.

Although I'd planned to have two of them, one on either side of our front door.

"Good," he said. "Now I won't have to worry about you going back to that house."

That, I assured him, was not on my future agenda.

Candy scampered after Crane as he climbed the stairs, but Misty still stayed at my side.

Now that I knew I was going to survive, my life went on as usual. Tomorrow was Sunday, which meant I had a whole day before I had to face my classes with a semblance of enthusiasm and energy for the day's work. A day of going nowhere and doing nothing except preparing dinner. I intended to let my school work slide.

Next week, as soon as I felt up to it and had a few free hours, I wanted to discuss my experience with Miss Eidt. In light of what had happened to me in Scarecrow House, perhaps she would be willing to part with some of its secrets.

Thirty

On Sunday, Brent stopped over for a quick visit. While we snacked on leftover pizza, he said, "I took the opportunity to go back to Scarecrow House and look around."

"How did you get in?" I asked.

"Easy. When we left, I didn't shut the door all the way."

Crane nodded his approval. He never worried about Brent.

"Did you find anything useful?" he wanted to know.

"No one was there. No surprise. I did see blood on the second floor. A trail leading to the bathroom."

"Hmm. I don't remember blood. I must have stepped right over it."

Strange. You'd think I would have seen it when I saw the telltale straw.

"It's obviously not Misty's blood," I said. "She must have really hurt my attacker."

I'd have added 'good girl, Misty,' but that would have brought her racing to the table. Along with Candy and Star, she lay in the kitchen with a clear view of the proceedings.

"One of the rooms on the second floor is being used as a sort of sewing room," Brent said. "There's a table with scissors and paints. There are boxes full of material all around and bales of straw."

That would have been one of the rooms I'd missed.

"Someone is assembling scarecrows there," I said.

"That would be my guess."

"That gives me an idea. Could my attacker have been a woman?"

"Who says a man can't make a scarecrow?" Crane asked.

"No one. I didn't see who hit me, but I've been thinking it was a man."

I was assuming the scarecrow maker and my attacker were the same person, which was moving too fast.

"How does Mac plan to find the person who hurt me?" I directed the question to Crane.

"First, he'll see if there's any DNA on that scrap of material Misty tore off him."

"And if there is?"

"Then we have him—if his fingerprints are on file. I wish we could ask Misty," he added.

"We can ask, but don't expect her to answer."

Hearing her name, Misty's ears stood up, then dipped back down. She licked her chops.

"Did anyone say anything about pizza?" I asked.

"I don't think so," Crane said.

The dogs didn't need to hear words when they could smell.

As for myself, I didn't want anymore. I started setting crust aside for them. Feeding crust to the collies was part of the fun of eating pizza, at least in my opinion.

~ * ~

I lay on the sofa resting for the remainder of the day. Although my head was still tender to the touch, the terrible pounding had gone. The rest of my body ached, though, as one would expect after a fall. I could deal with that.

Walking and fresh air helped. I took Misty, Halley, and Star for a short stroll up and down the lane, then hurried back to the sofa where memories of my harrowing experience derailed my hard-won peace of mind.

It occurred to me that I may have attracted the attention of the killer. If he or she were the anonymous person who had threatened Miss Eidt, perhaps more trouble was even now on its way.

The killer probably didn't know who I was or where to find me. I hoped. Let him believe I was simply a curious woman with a dangerous dog, someone snooping in a house that was supposed to be off limits to everybody except the homeowner. A woman with a thick skull who'd survived a blow meant to kill her.

Or disable her so he could make his escape. Surely if he intended to kill me he would have done a better job.

Still, I'd better lie low for a long while.

With leisure time to spare, I had long phone conversations with Leonora and Sue Appleton. I would have talked to Miss Eidt, too, but my message went to her answering machine.

It wasn't like Miss Eidt to be away from home on a Sunday as this was her one day to rest and read for her own pleasure. I hoped she was all right.

Don't find anything ominous in that, I ordered myself.

Perhaps she turned her phone off on Sundays to make sure she had an uninterrupted day. As I didn't normally call her at home, I wouldn't know.

~ * ~

On Monday, I was more or less back to my normal self. I sent Crane off to his patrol with a good breakfast, made my lunch, and gathered my school books, ready for another challenging day at Marston High School.

It was Leonora's week to drive, which meant I had an hour before I needed to concentrate. I planned to give my mind a rest, but no sooner was I in the car than Leonora wanted to hear what had transpired at Scarecrow House for the second time. In telling the tale again, I added the few details Brent had gathered.

She leapt to the same ludicrous conclusion that I had entertained in the first hazy moments after the attack.

"It must have been the scarecrow. He came alive. Right from the start, I knew they were evil."

"More likely it was the person who made him," I said.

"If you say so. I wouldn't go near that place again for a billion dollars. I still dream about scarecrows every now and then. What's odd is that I remember those dreams like they really happened."

"Are you still attached to a pole?" I asked.

"In the last one, I was hiding in a laboratory watching a doctor turn a woman into a scarecrow."

"Good grief. How did he do that?"

"He was wrapping a white cloth around her head and painting a face on it."

"Did you wake up screaming?"

"Almost. I felt like I couldn't breathe. In the dream, that is."

Not wanting to hear another nightmare tale, I commented on the red-gold-green autumn world in which we found ourselves. We traveled this way twice every weekday, but the woods always seemed to have a new vista to offer.

A respectable number of leaves still clung to the trees. One hard rain, one strong wind, and they'd all be on the ground. Although I loved living in a state where seasons changed, I felt sad at the prospect of saying goodbye to October.

Look forward to Halloween and Miss Eidt's party, I told myself.

If she still planned to have it. She hadn't mentioned it lately and hadn't added to the spooky decor in the library. The murder and the anonymous warning she'd received had apparently reduced her to a state of paralysis.

It was understandable. We were all living a real life fright these days: an old house where danger hid itself well, proliferating scarecrows, and a killer with an unknown agenda.

Who needed a special celebration?

Thirty-one

The classrooms of Marston High School could be another place of fright or a hallowed hall of learning. It varied and was never predictable.

Take my morning World Literature class, for example. Four days out of five, the students were well-behaved and even enthusiastic, and I was able to teach the day's lesson without disruption. The class was too good to be real. Which should have made dealing with an occasional altercation a breeze.

We were studying the structure of the short story, using as a model *3020*, a chilling depiction of a futuristic earth. The main characters were a pair of young time travelers. It was a cut above some of the other stories that held zero appeal for any reader, let alone tenth graders, even though someone, somewhere, considered them classics.

I thought my students were searching quietly for the story's climax, one of the questions on the day's worksheet. I was wrong. Abby, a petite girl with a blonde pixie cut, and Gail, another blonde with long straight hair, had been whispering nonstop in the back of the room while I helped another student, Peggy. I was waiting for her to understand what she was doing to reprimand them.

Without warning, a purse hit the floor, followed by an outraged shriek from Abby. Its contents spilled out into the aisle: A tube of mascara, a lipstick, a hairbrush, a candy bar, a pen. Abby glared angrily at Gail who regarded her with an insolent smile. All eyes were fixed on the whisperers-turned-combatants.

"What happened?" I demanded.

"She shoved my purse off the desk," Abby shouted.

"Prove it," Gail countered, winding a long strand of yellow hair around her finger. "It fell by itself."

"You did it on purpose. You bi—"

"That's enough," I said.

"But she *is* a—"

"Enough!"

As Abby bent down to retrieve her property, Gail knelt beside her and said sweetly. "Let me help." Whereupon Gail stamped the life out of the hapless candy bar. It was—had been—a Twix.

"Both of you, out!" I said. "To the office."

It was necessary to be specific. Otherwise, they'd choose their own destination which might well be out of the school.

They both stood, both assuming a fighter's stance.

"You'll be sorry, Gail! Just you wait. It was all her fault, Mrs. Ferguson."

"You're just jealous because—"

I broke in. "Tell it to Mr. Hallford."

Greg Hallford was the assistant principal, new this year. I hadn't had any reason to send discipline problems his way yet. He was rumored to be good with kids. Let him untangle the problem.

Abby gave Gail a shove that pushed her over on Brady's desk. Gail righted herself and grabbed a fistful of Abby's hair which was hard to do with Abby's short haircut.

"Leave the room, now!" I repeated. "Both of you."

They went, possibly to continue their hostilities in the hall. Brady, one of the more helpful members of the class, picked up the candy wrapper and dropped it in the trash. I'd have to mop the mess later before someone stepped in it.

Crisis averted. I took a deep breath. The incident wasn't over though. There might be a conference with the assistant principal and student, or even with the parent. Also, a teacher can't send a student to the front office without writing a disciplinary form. Usually, the student in trouble carries his own referral, but my two troublemakers had already gone through the door, slamming it on their way out.

I grabbed two forms from my desk and wrote: *Fighting in class. Over? Undetermined. It got physical.*

With luck, Grimsley wouldn't intercept it. These were the first two students I'd referred to the office this semester.

I handed the forms to Pamela, my student assistant who hadn't lifted her eyes from her book once during the entire drama.

"Take these to the office, please," I said. "The rest of us...back to work. Who knows where the climax of the story is?"

We were all happy to leave the unpleasantness behind.

"When they find out they can't get back to their own time?" Rosalie said.

"No." Ross waved his hand in the air. "That's a complication. I think the climax is where they find the crystal star. After that, the story's as good as over."

"I agree. The discovery of the star is the high point of the action. Anyone else?"

Silence met my query.

"Then let's move on to the resolution," I said. "At what point does the author wrap up all the loose ends?"

I waited for enlightenment and congratulated myself on defusing the situation. Except it had come with a price. A sinister throbbing began on top of my head where the assailant's weapon had landed its blow.

I should have taken another day to rest.

~ * ~

The following day, I drove us to Marston. After school, I wanted to stop at the library. Lenora wanted to go straight home.

It was another beautiful fall day, warm, but delightfully so with a fragrant breeze. Wisps of white clouds drifted across a vivid blue sky, and the many-colored leaves rustled.

I greeted Blackberry who presided over the porch in frosty silence from her favorite wicker chair. Pushing open the door, I looked for Miss Eidt.

Another bouquet, this one of deep pink roses, lent an air of graciousness to her desk. These looked as if they had come from somebody's garden. Miss Eidt, I remembered, grew roses behind the library.

Were the flowers a sign that she was at peace again? I only hoped so.

I found her in the Gothic Nook, taking paperbacks from a huge gathering basket and placing them on the shelves. She wore a deep pink dress as if to match her roses.

The candy dishes were empty, but true to her word she had brought out the house from the Apple Fair. She'd placed it under a Tiffany-style lamp whose dim yellow light gave it an appropriate ghostly cast. From the first, I'd known the Nook was the proper place for it.

"Did you have anything good?" I asked.

"Oh, hello, Jennet." She ran her finger across the crumpled cover of *To See a Stranger* by Margaret Lynn. "I read this one years ago. It's one of my all-time favorites. You'll love it."

I held out my hand. "No need to put it on the shelf then." I paused, then took the plunge. "I take it you haven't received any more anonymous messages."

"No. Maybe there won't be any. I was talking to Mac the other day. They don't have any leads in the murder. I'm afraid they're going to close the case."

"They won't do that. Not yet, anyway. It hasn't been that long. And something else happened."

The time had come for me to tell Miss Eidt about my misadventure at the Scarecrow House. By the time I mentioned Brent's discovery of the scarecrow making room, Miss Eidt had turned pale. The wary look was back in her eyes.

Congratulations, Jennet. You've killed her good mood.

Quickly, I segued to another topic. "How are plans for the party coming?"

"They're not," she said. "I don't think this is the year to have a party."

Oh, no! I was willing to bet the rest of the town was counting on it.

"I disagree," I said. "The timing couldn't be better. We could all use a little entertainment."

She set the remaining books on the table next to the mini-house and lowered herself into a rose-colored wing back chair.

"But think, Jennet. All those people wearing masks. We have a murderer in town. I say we'd be taking a chance."

"Discourage people from wearing costumes then."

But in a sense, she was right. At last year's party, I had been abducted by a masked man. If I could have seen his face, possibly I could have avoided the whole traumatic incident.

"That's half the fun," she pointed out. "I was looking forward to wearing my Queen of Hearts costume again."

"Let's take a chance that nothing will happen," I said. "And who knows? Maybe by Halloween, the police will have the case wrapped up."

Thirty-two

As we left the Gothic Nook, Miss Eidt gazed out over the library. All was quiet, which to her indicated that all was well. An elderly gentleman stood at the main desk holding a book from the nearby paperback carousel.

The word 'gentleman' slipped into my mind with ease. While most men dressed casually for a visit to the library, he wore gray slacks with a blue-and-white striped shirt and a tie. Silver strands threaded through his light brown hair, and his hand rested on top of a cane.

Automatically, I added the adjective dapper to gentleman, then handsome. Still handsome, I amended.

"I see I'm needed," Miss Eidt murmured. "He looks interesting."

"Very."

Curious, I accompanied her to the desk. I wasn't being nosy. I had to check out my book, didn't I? As I stood near the vase, the rich scent of roses wafted over me. I had a sudden irrational desire to help myself to one of them.

The dapper gentleman had a kind and winning smile. I couldn't say why, but he reminded me of Gilbert, Crane's uncle who had become Camille's husband. Perhaps he, too, was a Southern gentleman.

He set the paperback on the desk. It was Lucy Hazen's *Devilwish*. "Which one of you is the librarian?" he asked.

Miss Eidt laid her hand on the vase of roses. "I'm Elizabeth Eidt, the librarian."

"Allow me to introduce myself." He shook her hand gently but firmly. "My name is Chester Mayland. I need help finding books about houses."

"That's rather vague," Miss Eidt said.

"I should explain. I'm going to build a house in Foxglove Corners in the spring. In the meantime, I'm looking for inspiration."

"Would you like to see books with house plans?" she asked.

"If you have them. I want a house that will blend in with the existing architecture and still have distinctive features."

"That would be Victorian. We have several fine Victorians in Foxglove Corners. Do you want a large house?"

"Medium-sized. Two stories definitely. Not one of those ridiculous McMansions."

"I'm sure we can help you," Miss Eidt said. "Just give me a minute."

Quickly, she checked out *To See a Stranger*. "That'll be due in two weeks, Jennet. I'll see you before then."

"You will," I said.

Darn. Now I had no excuse to linger in the library and a few serious reasons to move on, but I wanted to know more about Chester Mayland. Specifically, had he already purchased acreage, and did he live in Foxglove Corners?

I couldn't intrude on their conversation. He'd hardly noticed me, only given me a fleeting glance.

Well, I wasn't the librarian.

I slipped my book in my shoulder bag. "Think about the Halloween party," I told Miss Eidt. "My vote is for having it and going ahead with the costumes."

She promised to do so, but her attention had already wandered. She smiled warmly at Mr. Mayland. "If you'll follow me, I may have what you're looking for."

It was obvious she found the dapper gentleman attractive. Perhaps he would prove to be a welcome distraction for her.

~ * ~

At home, I found Sue Appleton waiting for me on the porch. Halley and Misty kept their eyes on her from behind the window, but neither one was barking. They knew Sue well, even without her entourage of collies in attendance.

Sue was absorbed in her cell phone, smiling at something amusing she saw there.

I parked the car and joined her on the porch. "Were you waiting long?"

"About five minutes. It's such a beautiful day I felt like going for a walk, and I wanted to see you."

That was usually the prelude to rescue business.

"What's up?" I asked.

"You remember Tamryn Lynn wanted to join the Rescue League."

"Ah, the deluded one. You turned her down, though."

"Yes, with a letter. Well, she wrote *me* a letter. She wants me to reconsider. She says there's something I don't know."

"You're not going to reconsider, I hope."

"No, but instead of sending her another letter, I went to her house to talk to her in person. Her neighbor says she hasn't seen her for over a week."

"It was about a week ago when she stood me up."

"I wonder, would you stop over at her house in a day or two to see if she came back? I'd go myself, but I have a hundred and one things to do."

And I, of course, was a lady of leisure. But it was the easiest request Sue had ever tossed at me.

"I could drive by her house," I said, "but I don't want to talk to her."

"Just so I know. You don't even have to get out of your car."

The dogs began to bark. All the dogs. A deer appeared in the woods for a heartbeat, then disappeared into the thick foliage that grew at the edge. My prey-driven collies wanted to give chase. At least, some of them did.

"I'll do it tomorrow," I said.

"I'm not looking forward to this, but it has to be done."

"Do it, then it'll be over."

"Let's go in," Sue said.

"How'd you like a cold drink? I have fresh lemonade."

"That sounds good."

I opened the door, and we waded into a high wave of collies, leaping, barking, forgetting their company manners.

"Back!" I said. "Stay!"

All but Candy fell back. Rules and orders didn't apply to her, or so she thought.

"What a lively, lovely bunch," Sue said. She reached out to pat the nearest head which belonged to Candy.

"I love all collie colors," she said, "but there's something about a tri…" She didn't finish, didn't have to. She glanced at me.

Adept at reading her, I said, "Do you still have Velvet?"

"She's still at the ranch. I've had three people looking for collies, but they want puppies. As it turns out, we're getting three next week from an Ohio rescue."

"From the same litter?"

"The mother had six. Three are staying in Ohio."

"That's perfect," I said. "Three prospective puppy owners, three babies."

"But no one for Velvet," she added.

My poor little Apple Fair orphan. I didn't say anything. Didn't trust myself.

Seven collies swamping a visitor they all knew. How could I handle eight?

"Like I say," Sue repeated, "there's something about a tri."

I brought out two tall tumblers, filled them with ice, and set the pitcher of lemonade on the table.

"Camille sent over some sugar cookies shaped like bones," I said. "I thought they were for the dogs till she set me straight."

She'd delivered them in a wonderful new tin illustrated with a pair of collies, a tri and a sable. I turned around and almost stepped on Candy's foot.

I could read my black collie, too: *Refreshment time for you. How about for us?*

She danced out of the way and placed her long nose on the table. As Sue helped herself to a cookie, I opened the Lassie tin, and set out seven treats shaped like bones but made especially for dogs.

Seven. Not eight. A comfortable number.

Thirty-three

Miss Eidt was right about *To See a Stranger*. A good book makes a reader think. Whether the thoughts are deep or frivolous doesn't matter.

What if I woke up one morning, looked in the mirror, and saw a stranger's face looking back at me?

Letting my schoolwork slide, I read the book in one sitting after dinner that night. I simply couldn't wait until the next evening to find out how that was possible.

The author was Margaret Lynn. Her book had the potential to be a classic but had fallen through the cracks. I congratulated myself on having discovered it, and knew I'd be making another trip to the Gothic Nook to see if I could find her other books.

At the end of the next school day, I dropped Leonora off at her house and drove to the library. I was also curious about the dapper gentleman who planned to build a house in Foxglove Corners in the spring. Would Miss Eidt see him again?

I was primed for good news and optimism. What I found was Miss Eidt making a gallant attempt to pretend that nothing was wrong while her wary expression hinted at inner turmoil. She had pulled one of the roses from the vase and was shredding its pink petals. Poor rose. Poor Miss Eidt.

Her navy wool dress was so dark it might have been black, never a favorite color of hers, but it looked stunning with a single pearl on a long silver chain.

"What happened?" I asked.

"Anonymous struck again." She reached in a drawer and pulled out a folded paper. This one was printed in black magic marker in large capital letters.

YOU WERE WARNED NOW ITS TOO LATE ANONYMOUS

"Warned to confess to a crime I didn't commit," she said. "And too late. I'm afraid to think what that means. I called Lieutenant Dalby as soon as I found it," she added.

"Where was it this time?"

"In a book on the return cart. Like a bookmark with its edge sticking out so I'd be sure to see it."

"Did you see anyone suspicious loitering around your desk?"

"No one, but I was back in the Gothic Nook some of the time filling the candy dishes."

"With chocolates?"

"No, candy corn. In the spirit of the season."

A good sign followed immediately by a reason to be frightened. Again.

"Anonymous is getting ready to act," I said. "But until he does what can Mac do?"

She lowered her voice to a whisper. "He sent an undercover cop, Dale Mason, here," she whispered. "He looks young enough to be a high school kid. But I'm still worried."

I didn't see any young man who fit that description at the tables. Probably he was wandering through the stacks or patrolling the grounds.

"I would be worried, too," I said. "Why don't you go home? Better still, close the library for a few days and go somewhere relaxing. You never take vacations."

"The threat will still be here when I come back. I won't run away. This is my home."

And she wouldn't let anyone drive her from it. In her place, I would feel the same way.

"All because I wanted to buy a scarecrow," she said. "I wish I'd never gone back to that miserable house."

"It was unfortunate timing."

She pulled another petal from the rose while I seized on two telling words—'gone back.' She had visited Scarecrow House at some time in the past but wasn't ready to talk about it yet. I'd have to be patient.

"It was a bizarre coincidence, my being there just after the killer dumped the body in the field," she said.

As for myself, I'd gone inside Scarecrow House and Misty had taken a chunk out of him. Was I in danger, too? So far I hadn't seen any indication of it. Other than a blow on the head, that is.

That *was* a major indication. My head still hurt when I touched it or brushed my hair. But then, I'd ventured into that house of horror.

"I wish I could help," I said. "It's impossible to fight an invisible enemy. I can't even come up with a suspect list. Apparently, neither can the police."

Miss Eidt surveyed her library, her second home, her safe haven that was suddenly not so safe.

"He might be here this very moment," she said, "looking like an ordinary person. Bringing me a book to check out for him."

"You have police protection now," I pointed out.

"Except Dale can't follow me home." She swept the pink petals into a pile and gave her chain a light tug. "Just yesterday things were looking brighter. Do you remember Mr. Maywood?"

"Sure. It was only yesterday."

"Before he left, he asked me to have dinner with him this weekend. He said he wants to know more about Victorian houses in Foxglove Corners, but I wasn't born yesterday. It was an excuse to see me again. I haven't had a social engagement with a gentleman in...let's just say a long time."

"Go and enjoy yourself and forget about Anonymous. He's a coward, hiding behind notes."

"I will," she said, "and, Jennet, you'll be pleased to know I've decided to have the Halloween party after all, complete with costumes. I'm not going to let some faceless coward dictate my life."

I always like a challenge, especially one framed in a time limit.

"Let's try to draw him out in the open before Halloween. Now, I liked *To See a Stranger* so much, I want to read more books by Margaret Lynn. I saw on *Goodreads* that she wrote five. Do you have any?

"You'll have to look," she said. "Debbie plans to arrange the Gothics in alphabetical order, but that's a mammoth task. She got up to the C's and had to stop and do her regular work."

"I will," I said. "You know, that book cost fifty cents when it was new. Imagine."

She smiled. "Times change. The publisher, Ace, doesn't exist anymore. Fortunately, there are estate sales and bookstores."

Before the Gothic craze died out, Ace had produced hundreds of Gothic paperbacks, many of which were still out there. I just had to find them. That, at least, was something I could do.

~ * ~

As I turned off Jonquil Lane into my driveway, I saw a sight that turned my blood to ice water. A scarecrow slouched lazily in the white wicker rocker, seeming to watch me as I parked the car. Inside, the dogs were barking. Three of them pawed at the front window. To greet me or warn me?

To warn me. One of the scarecrows had followed me to my home. I'd always suspected they were alive. I felt my heartbeat racing, throwing open the Ford's door, determined to toss the interloper into the trash before it could harm my loved ones.

That thought died a quick death. I was looking at my own scarecrow, the one that had been stored in the basement. I remembered Crane saying something about putting it on the porch. I was supposed to give it a new look.

But why? It looked good to me, realistic enough to give me a momentary fright.

Usually I entered the house by the back door. Today I walked around to the front porch, my Margaret Lynn paperback in one hand, the house key in the other. The collies in the window flew into a frenzy. They didn't appreciate changes in the routine.

Before going inside, I studied the scarecrow at close range. She had yarn for hair, a hat trimmed with fake flowers, impossibly long eyelashes, and an exaggerated red smile.

Her creator had painted a smug look on her canvas face. Smug and somehow unsettling. How could I improve on that?

See, I told myself. *You thought of your own scarecrow as a living thing.*

What did that prove? Only that I had scarecrows on my mind.

Like Miss Eidt, I was beginning to wish I'd never seen Scarecrow House, had driven on to the cider mill and never set this grim adventure in motion.

It was, of course, too late for regrets.

Thirty-four

The next day, I drove by Tamryn's house to see if she was home. After an especially trying day at Marston, I was eager to relax before a host of evening chores claimed my time, but I wanted to cross this particular chore off my list.

I didn't think Tamryn would be there. As I approached the house, however, I saw signs that someone had been busy. The leaves were raked to the curb, leaving lawn, walkway, and driveway clear.

Bringing the car to a stop, I surveyed the house. It looked neater, from the outside anyway, but the drapes were still drawn across the window. I didn't see Tamryn's car or any other indication that she was in residence.

The house looked so bereft that, for a moment, I wondered if Tamryn would ever come back.

A tall woman came around the side of the brick ranch next door, rake in hand. Her beige pants were heavily stained at the knee indicating that she was nearing the end of a fall clean-up project. Here might be a source of information.

She was watching me, a half smile on her face, and a runaway leaf lodged in her gray-streaked blonde hair. Good. That suggested she was approachable. As I powered down the window, she walked up to the car, and pulled off her green gardening gloves.

"I've seen you here before," she said. "Are you a friend of Tamryn's?"

I decided to stretch the truth a bit. "You might say that."

"I'm Annabel," she said. "Tamryn and I have been neighbors for... oh it must be twenty years."

"Do you know where she is?" I asked.

"I haven't a clue. She didn't tell me. You're not the only one looking for her. Ben has been by twice."

"Ben?"

"Her ex-husband. He used to live here. Tamryn got the house in the divorce," she added.

You should have known that if you're her friend, she might have said.

Tamryn had never mentioned an ex-husband. She didn't wear a ring, but then why would she if she was no longer married? All we'd talked about was Cara and her conviction that she'd brought the dog back to life. Which inspired another question.

"Did Tamryn have a dog? A collie?"

Now Annabel looked suspicious, but she answered my question.

"Not anymore. She lost Cara a month or so ago. But here's something strange. One day I saw her lugging a big bag of dog food into the house."

"For the ghost dog?"

"What?"

I decided that Tamryn hadn't told her neighbor about Cara's appearances.

I said quickly, "She might be feeding strays."

"That could be. I know she throws out a soggy bread mixture for the birds every morning. But back to Ben, I wouldn't have given him any information about Tamryn even if I had any. She didn't want him to know anything about her. It wasn't a friendly parting. I just wish I knew what he wanted."

"Did you ask him?"

"I didn't. I don't want to get involved in their affairs. Besides, Ben was never very friendly."

"It's good of you to rake her leaves," I said.

"We can't let the neighborhood fall apart because one person neglects to keep up her property."

Annabel couldn't mask the disapproval in her tone. I felt the first stirrings of sympathy for Tamryn. What if she was somehow prevented from returning to the house by an accident, or heaven forbid, death?

A light breeze came up, and leaves blew across the street, a red and brown tidal wave. Annabel followed their progress with a bemused frown. "It's a never-ending battle."

Sensing that she was about to go back to work, I asked, "What about Tamryn's mail?"

"I've been picking it up," she said. "There hasn't been much, and she doesn't take a paper."

Under normal circumstances, when a homeowner has to be away for any length of time, he makes arrangements for someone to maintain his property. It only made sense unless he wants burglars to notice his house.

Was Tamryn in trouble? Had something unexpected come up after she'd sent her application to Sue?

"Will you let me know when she shows up?" I asked. "I'd really like to talk to her."

I jotted my phone number on a slip of paper I found in my purse.

"Sure," Annabel said, "*if* she shows up. Don't hold your breath."

~ * ~

Home was predictable. Once I entered the green Victorian farmhouse on Jonquil Lane, I knew what to expect. Collies vying with one another to lead the welcoming committee, dinner to plan and cook, a husband about to end his long patrol of Foxglove Corners. A long romantic evening. All good things with no surprises to alter the status quo.

No wonder my home was the one place I yearned to be when I was at Marston or any other place, for that matter. I was happy here and safe.

Crane was early, bringing in tokens of a windblown autumn with him. Literally. In his wake, a rush of crinkled maple leaves flew inside, and transferred themselves to collie coats.

The dogs, excited by his arrival, jumped on him. Well, not all of them. Halley was too dignified and well-mannered to indulge in wild dog behavior, and Sky was too timid. Raven, not wholly recovered from her broken leg, moved slowly. That left four leaf-covered whirling dervishes in the doorway.

For a moment, I tried to imagine an eighth collie, a little tri girl appropriately named Velvet, in the middle of the pack. I realized I wanted her to be there.

Don't disturb the *status quo*, my pestiferous inner voice whispered. *Don't meddle with perfection. Above all, don't let Crane know what you're thinking.*

Crane. His kiss still had the power to turn my blood to the boiling point. *Later*, I thought, when I have him to myself.

He waded through collies, bestowing pats on all seven heads. "How was your day, honey?" he asked.

"At school, chaotic as usual, but I learned a little more about Tamryn. Interesting stuff."

"Is she the lady with the magic ashes?"

"That's Tamryn. She wanted to join our Rescue League."

"Does anyone think that's a good idea?"

"Not at all. Anyway, she seems to have disappeared."

"She can't be serious about joining Rescue then."

"It's a mystery," I said.

"Another one."

While he locked his gun in the cabinet, I told him what I'd learned from Annabel. "Now I wonder if Tamryn had a good reason to be gone when I visited her."

"You won't know until she shows up," he pointed out.

"I guess not."

But I could speculate.

Living alone, had Tamryn slipped over the edge and re-created her lost dog for company?

When I first came to Foxglove Corners, I'd lived alone, too, with one dog. It never occurred to me to be lonely, not with a mystery in the yellow Victorian across the lane and a growing romance with a handsome deputy sheriff.

But if I'd lost Halley? What then?

In those days, Halley was young. I never gave a thought to her inevitable departure. I surely wouldn't think I could bring her back to life. Nor would I want to. She would be different, perhaps in a horrible way.

Tamryn and I were vastly different people. Thank heavens for that.

It occurred to me that Annabel hadn't seemed particularly curious about Tamryn's whereabouts. She raked her leaves to keep the neighborhood from looking neglected. Ben, the ex-husband, possibly had his own agenda.

As far as I knew, that left only me to worry about Tamryn. And Sue Appleton.

~ * ~

Something had been tugging at me, the kind of detail that lodges in your mind for a moment, then slips away to resurface at some future time when you're doing something else. Like blowing out the candles after dinner.

Tamryn had mentioned a friend, a man who thought she was out of her mind to believe that Cara had returned from the dead. His name wasn't Ben but something with two syllables. I couldn't remember it.

But I found that I could recall the conversation. Tamryn's boyfriend didn't believe in Cara. Therefore it was important to her that I did.

"Why?" I'd asked.

"Because if no one believes in Cara, she'll go away again."

It was the sort of comment that pushed the chill factor up a notch, which accounted for the fact that I'd almost forgotten it.

The point was that Tamryn wasn't alone in the world as I'd assumed. If her ex-husband was out of her life, another man was in it, someone who didn't share her illusion, who, in fact, ridiculed it. She might be somewhere with him at the moment, not having considered it necessary to inform her neighbor of her plans.

In which case, we didn't have to worry about her. But there was no way to know for certain, and a troublesome question lurked behind my theory. Who sends in an application to the Rescue League, then leaves town on a holiday?

Thirty-five

Dressed in black, I wandered through the throngs of costumed revelers who had flocked to Miss Eidt's Halloween party. With a tall pointed hat, a charcoal-colored midi-dress, and neon green nail polish, I thought I made a glamorous witch.

But something was wrong. Not with me. With the gathering.

The turn-out was greater than anticipated, but curiously, there was no noise, neither conversation, nor laughter, nor music. Not even the wail of the wind machine. Everyone had donned a costume. Knights in shining armor, cowboys, and clowns moved from the buffet table back into the crowd, pressing against me with insubstantial bodies. I saw rather than felt them.

As Queen of Hearts, Miss Eidt reigned over the festivities. Her long ball gown was black rather than the traditional red. Even her flashy Valentine jewelry was black, and her choker necklace consisted of black pearls. As for the cat, Blackberry, she was white. She sat on Miss Eidt's desk, jewel eyes glowing, appearing three times her actual size.

Miss Eidt's gentleman friend, Mr. Chester Maywood, stood proudly at her side. He was decked out like a riverboat gambler, complete with pistols. The blue drink in his champagne flute gave off lightning sparks. How odd.

I was afraid. None of this was natural. It wasn't right. It was… What? Reality twisted into a nightmare sequence.

I had to leave while I could. Turning quickly, I barreled into a person in a scarecrow costume. This was the one reveler who spoke. "I've been waiting for you, Witch."

The voice was hollow, like an echo. I couldn't tell whether the speaker was a man or woman, but the tone was unmistakable, deep and threatening.

"Time's up. You're coming with me."

With a straw hand, he reached for my waist. I pointed my witch's cane at him and laughed as his straw caught fire.

"Not in your lifetime," I said and watched him burn—

And woke, convinced I was smelling smoke. I wasn't, of course. What I smelled was a scent of applewood drifting over from the fireplace. After dinner, Crane had built a fire.

I was sitting in the rocker. *Whispers of Darkness* had fallen to the floor. Misty lay sleeping at my feet. Crane sat on the sofa reading the *Banner* while I attended a party without him, set fire to a scarecrow and watched it burn. Only in my dream. Still, a dream can reflect reality.

Maybe I shouldn't have talked Miss Eidt into going ahead with the Halloween party. With everyone in costume, how could one tell an innocent guest from a villain?

My throat was dry. You'd think I'd been inhaling real smoke. Seeing my cup of cocoa on the side table, I took a sip to find it tasted more like chocolate malted milk.

I couldn't have been asleep for long, about fifteen minutes, but what a vivid dream I'd had! No, a nightmare. A horrible nightmare.

Crane set the paper aside. Seeing that he was finished, Misty stirred and gave a piteous whimper. It was time for the dogs' last trip outside before bed. She started a chain reaction. The collies emerged from their favorite dark corners and congregated around Crane.

"Did you finish your book?" Crane asked.

"No, I fell asleep."

"That scarecrow lady's ad is back in the paper," he said. "Do you want to call her?"

"Definitely."

He rose and the collies followed him to the side door.

I glanced at the clock. It was late and tomorrow was a school day, but after my short nap I was wide awake. If it wasn't past eleven o'clock, I would have called Gwendolyn Larkin.

While Crane was outside with the dogs, I pondered this new lead. If her ad appeared in today's paper, presumably she intended to answer her phone. She might know who had access to Scarecrow House. I still hoped to find out who had dealt me that terrible blow. To encourage her confidence, I should buy one of her scarecrows. Even though I no longer wanted one.

~ * ~

I called Gwendolyn Larkin the next day during my lunch period. Luck was my side. After four rings, I heard a human voice, not a recorded message.

"Art by Gwendolyn," she announced. "May I help you?"

At last. "Ms. Larkin, my name is Jennet Ferguson," I said. "I'm calling about your ad for homemade scarecrows. I'd like to order one."

"In time for Halloween? I'm sorry. I'm in a bit of a time crunch."

"It doesn't have to be ready for Halloween. I plan to use it as a fall decoration."

"Well then," she said, "I can provide you with a custom-made scarecrow. When can we get together to talk about what you'd like?"

"As soon as possible. I'm in school until three, then I have an hour's drive back to Foxglove Corners."

"I know how that is. I'm a teacher myself. I teach middle school art."

Time was always a consideration. I'd already used five minutes of my short lunch period.

"How does Thursday sound?" she asked. "About six o'clock?"

"Perfect," I said.

"You have the address."

I glanced down at the ad. The address was South Pine Road. For a moment, I wondered if Ms. Larkin had a connection with Scarecrow House after all. I asked her.

"My uncle owns that house," she said. "He bought it as an investment but hasn't been able to renovate it yet. He let me display my spring collection on the property."

"Then you don't make your scarecrows there?"

"No, I work at home."

"You must know about the body found behind the house a few weeks ago," I said.

"I heard about it, yes."

Not, "I talked to police about it."

"It has nothing to do with me," she added.

"Okay. I'll see you on Thursday.

Now I had to hurry to finish my sandwich before the bell rang.

~ * ~

Leonora had stayed in her classroom and was almost through eating. She was unwrapping a brownie.

I slipped into a student desk and brought out my sandwich—deli turkey on whole wheat.

"Was your scarecrow maker in?" she asked.

"Yes, I'm meeting her after school on Thursday."

"That's tomorrow. I'll drive myself then. I brought you a brownie," she added.

"Thanks."

A quick glance at the clock told me I'd have to eat it during my conference hour. I swallowed, took another bite. It couldn't be healthy, gulping down my food like this.

"I don't know why you're still interested in those old scarecrows after getting hit on the head by one," Leonora said. "I think you'd want to keep your distance.

"My attacker wasn't a scarecrow."

"It was someone connected to them then."

I'd told her about Miss Eidt's anonymous notes and my own unintentional involvement in whatever was going on.

"It's a matter of striking before I'm struck."

"All I know is you're in danger again. Just be careful."

"Always," I said, and the bell rang.

~ * ~

Fifth period World Lit could be a difficult class to work with or a pleasure. It depended on certain factors I could never nail down. After the comparative freedom of lunch with the last class of the day beckoning, attention spans tended to shrink.

We were taking a break from the text. The assignment was to write a short short story set in the future. I set the limit at a thousand words.

"A thousand words!" cried Jerome, pushing his glasses up into his brown buzz cut. "We're kids, not writers."

"You're writing students," I said. "You have imaginations. Let them take over. Think of it as four typewritten pages, double spaced," I added.

That sounded like a lot. "Or less."

Reactions were mixed. A few students, the achievers, pulled paper from their notebooks and sharpened pencils. Work to be graded had to be written in ink according to English Department rules, but these were to be rough drafts.

"Let's brainstorm," I said. "What will the world be like in, say, a hundred years?"

"Just like it is now," said Jody. She had already written something on her paper.

"Overpopulated," countered Ella. "Like in *Soylent Green*."

That movie had left a vile taste in my mouth, but that was irrelevant. Overpopulation was a definite possibility.

"Maybe they can manufacture food," I said. "How about transportation?"

Max, ever polite, raised his hand and waited to be called on. "We'll all have space ships instead of cars."

Suddenly, answers were tumbling over themselves:

"And machines to bathe and dress us."

"And no school. We'll take a learning pill instead. Just think. A pill for Algebra One."

"Robot vacuums."

"We already have those, dummy," said May. "My mom has one."

"No name calling," I said. "Good ideas."

Just as I was thinking that I'd like to have one of those robot vacuums, too, the door opened and Grimsley sauntered in. He chose a vacant desk in the row by the windows. Without a word. That was his way. But this was good. We were discussing, engaged, learning.

I'd invited him in to witness my English lit students assume their Chaucer characters. He hadn't taken me up on that offer.

Glancing around the classroom, I hoped everything would go well today.

Well, Ally was adding a coat of lipstick to her dark red lips, and Sandra, unimpressed by Grimsley's presence, was reading her library book.

We had thirty minutes of class left, and with my luck, Grimsley would stay for all of them. If only we could all remain civil.

Thank the patron saint of teenaged students, we did.

Thirty-six

I should have given more thought to my special-order scarecrow. Well, purchasing one of Gwendolyn Larkin's wares was merely an excuse to talk to her. Still, if I was willing to pay for custom-made, wouldn't I want something distinctive?

"Just a scarecrow," I heard myself saying. "Like the one in *Wizard of Oz*."

First, I had to find Gwendolyn's house, a complicated matter as there were two Butternut Drives, east and west. No street light separated the two, but there was no traffic either. Entering West Butternut, I drove slowly in a shower of falling leaves, looking for Four-fifteen.

As it turned out, I needn't have worried about identifying the house. The porch of Gwendolyn's blue-sided bungalow was populated with brightly dressed scarecrows in all sizes. Two of them sat in lawn chairs. One lounged on the top step, leaning on a post. Still another looked as if it were about to knock on the door. She had included twins, dressed alike, and a mother and daughter group, the daughter being only three feet tall.

The display was attention grabbing, but a bit creepy. I wouldn't like to live across the street from her and see it every day.

Ceramic windchimes shaped like scarecrows moved fitfully in the light wind. The path to the door was narrow, with scarecrows standing sentinel on either side. I rang the bell and listened to the melodious chimes. Ms. Larkin opened the door almost immediately. She must have been on the other side.

Clad in tight fitting jeans with a silky yellow tunic top, for a moment she reminded me of one of her scarecrows. The tunic was similar to the garments she'd given a few of her creations, and her hair, swept back in a long ponytail, was the color of straw. I thought she might be around my age.

"You must be Mrs. Ferguson," she said.

"It's Jennet," I shook her hand,

"Call me Gwendolyn."

"You have quite a family here," I said. "Are these for sale?"

"They could be. Mostly I use them to advertise my work. Come in. Sit down. We'll talk."

She ushered me into a small hall that led to a spacious living room.

Oh, good heavens. There were scarecrows inside, too: sitting in each of the twin wing chairs arranged on either side of the fireplace, and standing at a side table. One, wearing a maid's costume, appeared to push a vacuum. How on earth could anyone live this way?

I sat on a peppermint-striped sofa, thankfully free of scarecrows.

Gwendolyn stood over me. "Would you like a drink, Jennet? Coffee or I have fresh cider from the farmers' market."

"I'm fine," I said.

"All right. Let's get down to business." She pulled a small notebook out of her pocket. "What would you like your scarecrow to look like?"

I glanced at the lady behind the vacuum. I'd have to improvise and do it quickly.

"I don't want her to be scary."

"That's the point of a scarecrow, though, isn't it? To scare crows away?"

"I don't have any crows. I just want a nice, seasonal decoration."

"Okay, I'll make one with a happy face. And clothes?"

"Mmm. A pink and white checked gingham blouse with ruffles. For a girl."

"I can do that," she said. "What else?"

"Give her something to make her distinctive. A scarf or...Wait! I know! Make her a crown out of *papier-mâché*. Now, about the price?"

"For what you describe, a hundred dollars will cover it," she said.

Oh, good grief. So much money for something I didn't really want. But I couldn't back out now. I'd better hurry and start my interrogation.

"On second thought, maybe I'll have a glass of cider, if it's no trouble," I said.

"None. I'll have one, too. Making scarecrows is thirsty work. Sometimes I get straw in my mouth."

While she busied herself in the kitchen, I quickly formulated a few questions. When she returned, setting the cider on scarecrow-themed coasters, I said, "Aren't you afraid someone will help themselves to those scarecrows you keep at your uncle's house?"

"They haven't yet," she said. "It's not like you can see them from the road easily."

"I did. I found them one day when I was going to the cider mill. And I went back. I was absolutely fascinated by them. They were so real and every one was so different." I paused, then added, "In fact, I was there the day they found the body."

I'd decided not to mention Miss Eidt's name, as the newspapers had simply referred to a passerby drawn to the scene by the scarecrow display.

"How horrible for you," Gwendolyn said.

"Yes, it was."

Aware that I was scrambling chronology, I said, "Someone removed the bride's veil. Then it was returned. I saw one of the scarecrows knocked over and one of them is gone. The point is, someone's been trespassing on your uncle's property. Or could it have been him?"

"Impossible. My uncle is home recovering from surgery. I promised him I'd keep an eye on the house, but I haven't been over there lately." She gestured toward her living room scarecrows. "So much to do...I like to stay home and do it."

"Does anyone else have access to the house?" I asked.

"Just my uncle and me. Why do you ask?"

I didn't want to mention that I was one of the trespassers but saw no way to avoid it. "One day while I was looking at the scarecrows, I saw that the back door was open. I heard moaning and thought somebody might be hurt. So I investigated."

Her stare began to cool, but she didn't say anything, simply took a swig of cider.

"And someone hit me on the head," I added.

"Someone? Who?"

"That I don't know. I didn't see him, didn't hear him approach."

"A vagrant must have broken in and made himself at home," she said. "I'll notify the police and make it a point to drive out to the house more often."

I saw no benefit to mentioning that Misty was with me, but there was something else she should know. "There's a room on the second floor where it looks like someone is making a scarecrow. It's filled with straw and jeans and paints."

"I'll accept the vagrant, but someone putting a scarecrow together in that old house...I can't believe that."

"It's true," I said. "You can see for yourself. I take it you don't know anything about that?"

In the pause that followed, Gwendolyn said, "You *do* want to buy a scarecrow, don't you? Or is this just an excuse to pump me for information?"

She had deftly avoided my question which suggested that she did know about the scarecrow room. But she was waiting for my answer, her stare growing progressively cooler.

"I want to buy a scarecrow," I said. "Of course I do. That's why I'm here. It's why I went back to the house on Mill Road to look at them. I left several messages for you," I added, thinking to throw her off balance. "They weren't answered."

She glided over that like an expert, took another gulp of cider and said, "I'll require a deposit."

"Will twenty-five dollars do?"

"Very well. I'll give you a call when your scarecrow is ready to pick up."

And no more talk about whatever is going on at my uncle's house, she might have added.

She pulled a pad from her pocket and hastily wrote a receipt. Handing it to me, she walked to the door. The visit was over. I hadn't finished my drink, but that didn't matter. Like the scarecrow, I hadn't really wanted it.

And what had I learned? Not much. On the contrary. I had more questions.

Thirty-seven

On the way home, I replayed my visit to Gwendolyn Larkin. Did Gwendolyn know who was assembling scarecrows in her uncle's house? Maybe. She hadn't seemed surprised when I mentioned it. Only annoyed, as if I'd discovered an enterprise she hoped to keep secret.

That didn't make sense. Nor did her indifference to the vandalism done to her work. She'd hardly reacted when I told her one of her scarecrows was missing and about the apparent theft.

Finally, and most important, did she have any knowledge of the body found lying amid her scarecrows? Probably not, or the police would consider her a person of interest at least. For all I knew, they did.

If I were Gwendolyn I'd have the locks changed on Scarecrow House. Unless she knew who the scarecrow maker was. I'd come full circle. I was leaving Jonquil Lane, turning in my own drive, and eager for another encounter with her.

My gaze fell on the scarecrow on the porch. It looked lonely, and suddenly I was glad it would soon have a companion, even at an exorbitant price. A royal companion. I'd thought of the crown at the last minute, even though scarecrows usually wear hats rather than crowns. This, however, was a custom creation. I could have anything I wanted.

Before discovering the house on Mill Road and its bizarre field, I'd never given scarecrows much thought, hadn't even brought our old one out of storage last Halloween. Now I seemed to be awash in them.

The dogs were barking. I'd stayed longer with Gwendolyn than I'd planned, and Crane would be home soon. As usual, I had no idea what to make for dinner, but a freezer full of possibilities. Grateful for a brief respite from mysteries, I unlocked the door, and was promptly set upon by leaping fur, wagging tails, and playful nips.

My dear ones were welcoming me home.

~ * ~

I was concerned about Miss Eidt and also curious about her romance with Chester Mayland—if romance was the right word. A dinner with a congenial man would be an improvement over waiting for Anonymous to strike again.

Miss Eidt had never seemed lonely to me, but she must have been, at least occasionally. Every day she dressed in a suit or dress, added pearl jewelry and stepped into a surround of books and fictional characters. If anyone could benefit from the companionship of a good man, that was Miss Eidt.

I was assuming Chester Mayland *was* a good man. One never knew.

She looked happy enough today with a serene smile and a touch of azure eyeshadow that matched the blue of her knit dress. I watched her place miniature pumpkins in the rooms of the dollhouse.

"How pretty," I said, marveling at the detail. Some stems were crooked as they would be on real pumpkins, and a few were already 'carved.'

"Debbie knitted them. She's a multi-talented young lady."

"I should say so. You're still having the Halloween party, I hope?"

"Debbie is making posters as we speak."

"And you haven't heard from Anonymous?"

"Not a word. Knock on wood." She rapped on the table that held the dollhouse.

"Thank heavens for that."

I set *Whisper of Darkness* on the desk. "It's not as good as *To See a Stranger,* but I enjoyed it. It's an old-fashioned Gothic."

Miss Eidt slipped the paperback into the return cart. "Did you dust off your witch's costume?"

"I just need to find my hat."

And my magic cane in case I want to set fire to a scarecrow.

Unbidden, fragments from my recent dream formed in my mind. Quickly, I shoved them back to oblivion.

Miss Eidt placed the last pumpkin on the tiny kitchen table and stepped back to admire her decor.

"How was your date?" I asked.

"It wasn't a date. At my age, we call it a social engagement." She moved the last pumpkin slightly to the right. "We had prime rib dinners and wine. Chester is so enthused about the house he's going to build that it was all he could talk about. It was a nice evening."

"It sounds better than nice," I said.

While we were talking, we'd been making our way to my favorite part of the library, the Gothic Nook where I half hoped to find another one of Margaret Lynn's books. The miniature house from the Apple Fair was still on the table, under the Tiffany style lamp, blending in perfectly with the other seasonal decorations as I knew it would.

"Look at this!" Miss Eidt frowned. "The candy dishes are already empty, and there are mashed chocolate cherries on the floor. Several of them. And here's a book right in the mess."

"Kids?" I murmured.

"I don't think so. As a rule, young people don't look for Gothics. They consider them old-fashioned."

That left adults.

"I suspect Natty Smith is up to his old tricks." She held her frown. "It looks like someone spilled out the chocolates deliberately and stamped on them."

"And what a waste of good candy. The poor book. It's sticky."

"It's ruined. Excuse me, Jennet. I'd better clean this up before somebody steps in it."

Usually, though, readers are respectful of books, I thought. Except for Natty. But Miss Eidt's ban on eating and drinking in the library was in place for a reason.

Avoiding the puddle of squished chocolates, I began to search for another Margaret Lynn Gothic and was soon so entrenched in my own world that I didn't realize I had company until a familiar voice said, "Hello, Jennet."

Edwina Endicott, ghost chaser, had joined me in the Nook. Edwina always seemed a little otherworldly to me, like a wraith herself in soft neutral colors that rendered her part of the background. Today, she wore off-white with an ivory lace shawl secured around her shoulders with a silver brooch. She held a stack of books in her arm.

"Edwina," I said. "Are you getting ready for a long rainy spell?"

She laughed. "This is just a typical week's reading. I thought I'd add a Gothic."

"That's always a good choice."

"Are you coming to the party?" she asked.

No need to ask what party. Only one mattered.

"I plan to."

"What are you going as?"

"A witch. And you?"

"I haven't decided," she said. "I want a costume that'll make me stand out in the crowd and maybe win a prize."

How unlike her.

"I'd like something romantic," she added. "I heard there was going to be a big surprise at the party this year."

"Oh?"

"Something really scary."

Scarier than swinging skeletons or green-faced vampires?

"Like what?"

"Nobody knows, but it's rumored to give new meaning to fright night."

"Where did you hear this?"

She shrugged. "Around."

"I wonder if Miss Eidt knows about it," I said.

"Well, she must, mustn't she? It *is* her party."

I doubted Miss Eidt had any knowledge of a Halloween night surprise. She wouldn't like that. She made her own plans and was a staunch believer in tradition.

If there were any truth to the rumor, however, it might mean that another person had a special plan for the party. And it wasn't necessarily good.

Thirty-eight

The next day, after a staff meeting tacked onto the end of the school day, Leonora and I decided to forgo cooking and buy dinners at Clovers. As a new bride, Leonora had balked at serving her husband, Jake, restaurant meals, but I had changed her way of thinking. As I had told her, Jake wouldn't know the difference, and he didn't. Besides, Clovers wasn't just any restaurant. Their meals were truly home-cooked and they included the best comfort food in Foxglove Corners.

Hemmed in by woods on three sides, Clovers had a thick carpet of multi-colored leaves on the ground. We had passed the peak color season and it wouldn't be long before the trees would be gaunt and bare. But this afternoon that day seemed far away.

I parked the Focus and we crunched our way up to the door while the wind threw swirling leaves in our path. As the clover chimes on the door announced our arrival, I looked toward my favorite booth and found it occupied by a red-haired man in a forest green shirt and camel vest.

"Brent's here," I said.

He waved to us and shouted, "Come join me." Several heads turned in our direction. He sprang up to take our jackets and hang them on a hook. "Did you girls have to stay after school?"

"We did," Leonora said. "For talking in class."

"Funny."

He hadn't received his food yet, only black coffee in a mug with his name emblazoned on it in gold letters.

"Good news," he said, pushing the evening edition of the *Banner* toward me. "Look what I just read."

The headline on the second page fairly screamed at me: *Scarecrow Killer Strikes Again*. I read the short article out loud.

An alleged road rage incident on Spruce Road has left one driver dead and another in police custody. Angered at having to follow a slow-moving vehicle on a stretch of curving roadway, Ronald Akerman, thirty-one, of Maple Creek confronted James Vining, an off-duty policeman, at a red light. Akerman pulled out a gun and shot Vining in the chest.

Under questioning, Akerman confessed he was involved in a similar incident earlier in the month when he dragged his victim from his crashed car and dumped him behind a vacant house on Mill Road.

"That's our man," Brent said. "Now we know his name. He committed two murders."

"Scarecrow killer," Leonora murmured. "How appropriate."

She read the article again to herself. "I shudder to think of a maniac like that sharing the road with us."

"So it's over," I said.

One mystery solved. But not by me. That didn't matter as long as Akerman had been caught, but I couldn't help feeling a bit miffed. Why did I, married to a deputy sheriff with a friend in the Foxglove Corners Police Department, have to read about the apprehension of the killer in the paper?

"Now Miss Eidt doesn't have to worry about messages from Anonymous," Brent said. "He'll have to stop harassing her because obviously she isn't guilty of anything."

That sounded good but not quite accurate.

"But is it really over?" I asked. "Who's Anonymous, and why did he target Miss Eidt? It doesn't sound like Akerman."

Brent shook his head. "No, it doesn't."

"It was some busybody taking advantage of the situation then," Leonora said.

It appeared that Miss Eidt's messages didn't have anything to do with the body in the scarecrow field.

"I guess I'm safe now, too," I said.

"There was a more detailed account on the news," Brent said. "People who know Akerman claim he has a short fuse, especially when he's behind the wheel of a car. He doesn't sound like the kind of jerk who would threaten a harmless librarian."

I thought about it. "I agree. Or hang around a vacant house and bash me on the head. That means there's some other person out there who is up to no good."

"That's one way to put it," Brent said.

"That means I'm not safe."

"Why aren't you safe?"

"Because there may be two killers," I said.

"Another one?" Annica set an enormous platter of food in front of Brent, filet mignon on a bun surrounded by French fries, which reminded me of our reason for stopping at Clovers. Her crystal ghost earrings sparkled in the last light of the afternoon.

She glanced at her fellow waitress, Marcy, who nodded, a silent promise to cover for her, and sat next to Brent.

"Two killers?" she echoed.

Brent took a huge bite of his sandwich. "Don't borrow trouble, Jennet."

"Then can you explain my attack in Scarecrow House?" I said.

"You discovered a vagrant's hideaway? It just happened once."

"Because I've stayed away from there."

And I intended to avoid the whole of Mill Road from now on, even, unfortunately, the cider mill.

"Let's just be happy with what we have," Annica said. "The guy who dumped the body in with the scarecrows is behind bars. End of story."

It was a good plan. A satisfying plan. I decided to take Annica's advice.

"Let's talk about something fun like Miss Eidt's Halloween party. I've been wondering about my costume. Miss Eidt wants us to dress like characters from a book."

"I'm Robin Hood," Brent announced.

I smiled fondly at him, remembering all the good he had done. "Yes, you are."

"When I was a little girl, my favorite book was *Heidi*," Annica said. "I can be a Swiss miss with two long braids. What do you guys think?"

"That you'll be pretty," Brent said.

"Unless you want to go for seductive," I pointed out.

""How about you, Jennet?" she asked.

"I'll dress as a witch again," I said.

"That isn't a storybook character."

"Sure it is. The wicked witch from *The Wizard of Oz*."

"Oh, right. Leonora?"

"I haven't thought about it yet. I'll come up with something."

"Life can be so mundane, it'll be fun to set aside one night for pure fantasy," Annica said.

I wouldn't call life mundane, not my life anyway, but Annica was right. After the trauma of the past weeks, a Halloween party would be the perfect way to regain our collective equilibrium.

"I'd love to win the prize for the best costume," she announced.

"I hear it's a book," Brent said.

"Whatever."

I thought about repeating what Edwina Endicott had said about the big surprise and decided against it. No doubt the big surprise was all in her mind.

Thirty-nine

In the mood for Halloween reading, I took a quick trip to the library after school the next day. We had stories by Ray Bradbury in our World Literature textbook, but I recalled a collection titled *The October Country*. Our school library didn't have it, but Miss Eidt certainly would.

She had stocked the paperback carousel with seasonal favorites. As she also enjoyed the works of Bradbury, I suspected she'd have the book I wanted.

I didn't see her at her desk, but she must be around. In her office, perhaps.

After finding my book, I slipped into the Gothic Nook. Not seeing anything there to tempt me, I went back to the supernatural section. Nothing new there either. I might as well check out my Bradbury book and go home.

I turned in the narrow aisle that ran along the library's north side and gasped as a burly man barreled into me. He was small and chunky. His Star Trek Voyager shirt struggled to contain his bulk.

His book and a large paper cup went flying. A loose paper flew out and landed at my feet. In moments, a dark milky liquid spread over the book's soft cover, and a smell of coffee escaped into the air. The book absorbed the drink as if it were dying of thirst.

"Can't you watch where you're going?" Chunky snarled the question.

Wait! He had collided with me.

"I oughta make you buy me another coffee," he said. "Yeah. That cost me six bucks. Yeah. I'll do it."

Road rage in the stacks, I thought. *Keep calm.*

Still, I couldn't resist the urge to say, "Just try it. There's a rule against drinking in the library."

"Rule be damned. I'll try it all right."

Where was Miss Eidt? What happened to all the people I'd just seen? To Debbie? To Miss Eidt's policeman, for heaven's sake?

His expression shifted as he noticed the paper. Something told me to pick it up quickly. He tried to grab it out of my hand, but I'd already read the words printed on it:

MISS EIDT ITS TIME ANONYMOUS

"You're Natty Smith!" I cried. "You're the one who's been harassing Miss Eidt."

But I was talking to the air. Natty had turned tail and run like the coward he was, leaving behind a book soaked with coffee and a paper that identified him as the author of Miss Eidt's threatening messages, not to mention a stain on my skirt. Clutched tightly in my hand, *The October Country* had stayed dry.

Debbie came up behind me. "What's all the racket? Who made the mess?"

"Natty Smith," I said.

"That jerk. I thought Miss Eidt sent him packing."

"He came back."

Debbie picked up the soaked book, holding it gingerly. Cool coffee out of its container loses its all allure. It looked disgusting. Miraculously, the threatening paper had escaped the soaking.

"This book just came in," Debbie said. "All of these old books lying around. Why couldn't it have happened to one of them?"

"The important thing is that now we know who's been threatening Miss Eidt."

"That silly little man. But why?"

"My guess is to get even with her for banning him from the library. Not that he took it seriously."

And we'd assumed the threatener was the killer or a witness of Ross Morrow's murder. There was a lesson to be learned here.

Debbie stepped around the mess on the floor. "That's great news. Let's tell Miss Eidt."

"Another mystery solved," I said. "We're on a roll."

~ * ~

All Hallow's Eve.

Halloween night brought an unwelcome change in the weather. Rain expected to last throughout the evening.

I glanced at the array of perfume bottles on the dresser, wondering which one a witch would choose. How about *Autumn Song*?

Sound carried in the house. Raindrops splattering on the windows, the wail of the wind as it blew in from the north, Candy downstairs barking her displeasure. She sensed I was going out and she would be left behind.

It hadn't taken me long to transform myself into a witch. My costume was as easy to assemble as any outfit I wore to school. The black midi-dress was perfect for a Halloween party—or a funeral. I found an antique onyx ring in my jewelry box, and a pendant on a silver chain with a bright green stone.

A witching stone, I told myself. It brought out the green in my eyes, as did the green nail polish.

A fuzzy memory slipped into my mind. I had been to one Halloween party already—in a dream. I'd painted my nails green and things hadn't turned out well.

Misty brushed against me, leaving white hairs on my dress. Like Candy, she knew I was going out and wasn't taking her. Camille, who declared she was too old for Halloween parties, was going to babysit for me. Crane was on duty, but he promised to make a last stop at the library.

I brushed my bangs to one side and set the tall pointed hat on my head.

"You'll do," I told my mirror image.

I was leaving early. Leonora had volunteered to bake four dozen cupcakes for the party, and I'd offered to help her transport them from her kitchen to the library.

Don't forget to take your cane, whispered my inner voice, as always trying to be helpful. *You might need it to start a fire.*

What cane? I didn't own a cane. Besides, witches carried broomsticks.

Undaunted, the voice added, *Take the umbrella then. You'll definitely need that.*

I agreed. I rummaged in a downstairs closet for the umbrella, poured fresh water for the dogs, and fed them an extra ration of peanut and banana treats in honor of the evening. Then I left the house quietly, confident that the collies would settle down. The prospect of a pleasant evening of pure fantasy (Annica's words) beckoned. I was more than ready for a good time.

~ * ~

Thunder in the north added to the evening's ambience. I carried the first tray of cupcakes up the steps to the library's porch while Leonora searched for a parking place in the crowded lot.

In keeping with the night's theme, Blackberry wore a wide orange ribbon. She shared her wicker chair with a jack-o'-lantern whose bright faux candle threw the surrounding decorations into shadows.

Setting the tray on a side table, I opened the door and stepped into a vestibule festooned with cobwebs. Part of the decor, I felt certain. As I retrieved the tray, Brent waded through a curtain of orange and black streamers, resplendent in his Robin Hood attire.

His costume looked like the clothing he wore for fox hunting: A lot of green and brown, suede and leather, camel vest and boots. His dark red hair had a shine in the dim party lighting. "Let me help you with that," he said. "What's under the cloth?"

Leonora had covered the baked goods to protect them from the rain. "Cupcakes decorated in Leonora's own kitchen." I handed him the tray. "Leonora's right behind me. If you take these to the buffet, I'll go back for another tray."

But first, I couldn't resist looking in at the party. In spite of the rainy weather, at least a hundred people had donned costumes and come out to celebrate the evening. There was muted music—an unfamiliar antique air—conversation, and laughter. Everything the dream party had lacked.

"Incoming," Leonora announced. She wore a plain white dress, and an authentic nurse's cap borrowed from her great-aunt covered her bright blonde hair. An old man in a waist-length gray beard held the door for her.

Rip van Winkle?

Miss Eidt, an enchanting Queen of Hearts in red and white, eyed the tray. Leonora set it on the buffet table and whipped off the cloth. She had outdone herself, creating faces on the cupcake tops: witches, pumpkins, ghosts, and black cats sculpted on mounds of chocolate and vanilla frosting.

"Perfect!" Miss Eidt said. "These won't last long. Thank you so much, ladies. Everybody's been so helpful. Brent brought the cider, and Lucy's going to read tea leaves. I just settled her in the Gothic Nook with a supply of orange pekoe and an electric teakettle. She donated a hundred copies of her books for party favors," she added.

"Is Mr. Maywood here?" I asked.

"He's somewhere, dressed as a cowboy from a Zane Grey book I never heard of."

I took another look at the party goers. Everybody appeared to be having a good time. This was one of the rare instances when the denizens of Foxglove Corners gathered together.

Miss Eidt lowered her voice; I could barely hear her. "I thought about opening the secret room but decided against it."

"That would be a star attraction," I said.

Although Miss Eidt had grown up in the library when it was her family's home, she had been unaware of the secret room. After the ghost girl who haunted the library had been laid to rest, she had opted to keep the room secret. Today, it was again well hidden. Few people were aware of its existence.

"You can do that next Halloween," I said.

"I agree. I think this year we have enough."

Leonora set the last tray on the table and began to arrange cupcakes on an orange paper platter. They were so colorful, so expertly decorated, that it was a shame they were destined to be eaten.

As I told her what Miss Eidt and I had been talking about, a crash of thunder rolled across the library.

"Is that the storm?" Leonora asked.

"It's Brent's CD," Miss Eidt said. "It's called *Sounds for a Haunted Holiday.*"

"If this rain keeps up, we may have the real thing," Leonora said.

"That's all right for us. It's a shame for the trick-or-treaters, though."

Miss Eidt helped herself to a ghost cupcake topped with two chocolate chips for eyes. "I'm glad I decided to go through with the party. I just hope we don't run out of refreshments."

I didn't think that was likely to happen. She and Debbie had pushed three of the library's tables together, and every inch of it was covered with something wonderful to eat or drink.

"Brent brought a hundred doughnuts from the Hometown Bakery, just in case. Go mingle, Jennet. Have fun. The night is young."

I was eager to do that. Leonora was still fussing with the arrangement on the buffet table. I ladled cider into a paper cup and headed for my favorite destination, the Gothic Nook. If I didn't have my tea leaves read, the evening would be incomplete. Besides, I wanted to say hello to Lucy and bring her up to date on developments in the mysteries.

Brent stepped out from the stacks. "Your hat is crooked, Jennet."

"Thanks." I reached up to straighten it. It was also damp.

"Is everything all right?" he asked.

"Why wouldn't it be? Do you expect trouble?"

"Not exactly, but—"

"But what?"

"I promised the sheriff I'd keep an eye on you until he gets here."

"What does he think is going to happen?"

"Anything. Remember last Halloween."

I wasn't about to forget it. Having been snatched by a kidnapper, I'd missed most of the party.

"That was last year," I said. "This year's villain is in jail. Besides, I can defend myself. I have poison."

I tapped a tiny flower and the onyx ring opened to reveal the dab of white powder inside. "It's a poisoner's ring. Annica sold it to me when she worked at Past Perfect. If anyone threatens me, I'll tip the contents into their drink."

Brent bent down to get a closer look. "That white stuff is poison?" he asked. "Arsenic?"

"Actually, it's lily of the valley dusting powder, but that's my secret."

"Nice, but not very effective if somebody attacks you. You have a way of attracting trouble. I'm quoting the sheriff. Anyway, I'm Robin Hood. My job is to keep the peace."

"That's not how I remember the story," I said.

"This is pure fantasy night. We can rewrite events. I'm quoting Annica now."

I was seriously annoyed at the condescension of the men in my world. However, Crane meant well, even if he was over-protective, and certainly Brent took his role of protector of the helpless—and women—to heart.

Who knew? The time might come when I would be glad to have Brent on my side. After all, my poisoner's ring was only for show.

Forty

Lucy sat at a round table in the center of the Gothic Nook. It contained perhaps a dozen plain white teacups and an electric teakettle. She wasn't wearing a costume, but her usual all-black attire, gold chains and Zodiac charm bracelet served as one.

A poster attached to a shelf announced: *Fortunes by Lucy*.

At present, she only had one customer, Annica, whose red-gold hair was concealed under a blonde wig with two long braids. Annica looked charming and demure and happy. She must have a good fortune.

"Hey, Jennet, I'm going to find my true love tonight," she said.

"You'd better get busy then."

"See you around," she said. "I'm going to look for Brent."

"You're next, Jennet," Lucy said. "The water just boiled."

She brewed a fresh cup of tea, and I took the seat Annica had vacated.

I sipped the tea slowly, grateful for a moment to rest. Carrying trays is hard work.

"I have a bad feeling about tonight," Lucy said.

"Oh, no. Bad for me."

She shrugged. "It could be."

A crash of thunder underscored her words. I couldn't tell if it came from outside or from Brent's Halloween CD.

"Is it that I won't find my true love tonight?" I asked.

She laughed softly. "It's easy to make Annica happy. Seriously, maybe it's the weather; maybe it's the unusual surroundings. Evil may lurk behind a mask. I don't like it, Jennet."

"Not everyone is wearing a mask," I pointed out.

She nodded. "Only Evil. Goodness doesn't hide itself."

Lucy's grim comments almost convinced me to skip the reading and just enjoy a chat with her and a cup of tea. Almost.

She had read my tea leaves countless times, and often repeated herself. She frequently saw an initial 'C' (Crane) near my home. I was going to take a trip, which hadn't happened yet. I had an overflowing basket. That could only mean endless happiness which was certainly welcome.

Why would tonight be different?

"Evil seeks out the vulnerable," Lucy said.

"Evil got caught shooting an off-duty police officer," I told her. "There's no danger from him anymore."

"So I read. But Evil has a large family."

"Let's hope they stayed home tonight. Now for that tea—"

Wishing I'd brought a cupcake to eat with my tea, I soon drained the cup, pouring excess liquid into the saucer. I knew the procedure. Three times around, make a wish, the spell's wound up. I handed my cup to Lucy and waited.

She took what seemed like a long time studying the symbols created by the formation of the leaves. At last she said, "I see an overflowing basket and a heart in your home. See." She pointed to a leaf that resembled a lopsided Valentine.

That was encouraging, but it was what she didn't say.

"That's all good," I said. "What else?"

"I also see...Now, I don't want you to worry, but to me, this long leaf looks like a scarecrow."

In my opinion, more than one leaf looked like a scarecrow. Or a tree or a figure or a vintage rocketship, for that matter.

I took back my cup and studied the symbol, but I lacked whatever talent allowed Lucy to interpret it. She knew about Leonora's and my adventures in Scarecrowland. She even considered using our experiences in a new book. And she knew how I'd been assaulted at the house on Mill Road.

A woman in a long white dress with a matching cloak entered the Gothic Nook, waited for a moment, then turned to leave.

The Woman in White. Who else?

"Come in," I said. "I'm just leaving."

"If you're sure—"

"I am."

"Be careful, Jennet," Lucy said. "Stay away from all evil things."

The woman stared at her, no doubt wondering if Lucy was more than a reader of tea leaves and a writer of horror novels.

To the newcomer, she said, "Is orange pekoe all right?"

~ * ~

Beyond the confines of the Gothic Nook, the number of partygoers appeared to have doubled in size. Meanwhile, in another part of the forest, Robin Hood found himself trapped by the wiles of Scarlett O'Hara. He looked uncomfortable, and she didn't appear to be in a hurry to move on.

Her costume looked so authentic it might have been sewn by hand. She brought to mind the opening scene in Gone *with the Wind*—Scarlett at the Wilkes' barbeque at her flirtatious best with one beau instead of two.

Only this Scarlett's long, wavy hair was a rich red, the shade called titian, and she looked familiar. No mystery here. The southern belle was Alethea Venn, Brent's friend from the Hunt Club, the woman who considered him her private property. The one I'd never liked.

Who would have thought Alethea would come to a party at the town library? She linked her arm with Brent's.

Ah, the suspense grows!

From a little way apart, Annica watched them. Then, apparently reaching a decision, she walked quietly up to them. Little Heidi ready to take on the South's prime flirt.

I wasn't close enough to them to hear what she said, but that could be remedied. I moved nearer to the trio, fully intent to eavesdrop, only to feel something brush against my leg.

Turning, I saw an elderly lady in a shapeless blue house dress with a long apron tied around her waist. Her gray hair had a tight curl and bluish tinge, and she wore an unfashionable pair of wire-rimmed glasses.

She had a dog with her, a small black collie on a leash. Around her neck the dog wore a bandana that identified her as Big Bad Wolf.

"Trick or treat," the woman said.

I stared at her, recognition slowly dawning.

"Sue? Sue Appleton? Is that you? And Velvet? Good grief, Sue, you look thirty years older."

"It's amazing what a little makeup can do, and I'm wearing a wig."

"Did Miss Eidt say you could bring a dog to her party?"

I bent down to give the bouncing little collie the caresses she'd been begging for.

"I can if she's part of my costume," Sue said, "and if I keep her away from the refreshments. Hence the leash. Velvet is the Wolf. Diane came with me. She's little Red Riding Hood. We're a three-woman team."

"Where is Diane?" I asked.

She was one of the two girls who helped Sue at her horse farm.

"Off somewhere with Debbie," Sue said. "We plan to win a prize. I had another reason for dreaming up this costume," she added. "I want to give Velvet a little exposure, and it's working. Four people asked if they could take our picture. Then I tell them I'm with rescue."

Velvet looked adorable. Surely someone here tonight would see that and hear she was available for adoption, which was what we wanted.

Didn't we?

"Have you been out in the garden?" Sue asked.

"No, it's raining."

"It stopped. The garden is beautiful. Absolutely unearthly. There are hundreds of pumpkin lights all around, and there's a skeleton in the fountain."

"A skeleton?"

"Not a real one," she said quickly. "It was one of Brent's ideas. Sort of ghoulish, don't you think?"

"For a Halloween party, not really."

I looked for Brent, Alethea, and Annica, but couldn't see them in the crush. I was dying to know who had prevailed. I suspected Annica was no match for Alethea.

Between Annica and Alethea, Brent wasn't living up to the promise to keep an eye on me.

Oh, well, I could take care of myself.

"Did you see anyone wearing a scarecrow costume?" I asked.

Forty-one

"A scarecrow costume?" Sue repeated. "Everybody's supposed to dress like a character in a book."

"There's a scarecrow in *The Wizard of Oz*."

"Oh, yes. Well, I didn't see any. Why?"

"Just wondering," I said.

Lucy had seen a scarecrow in my cup, but it didn't necessarily have any evil intentions toward me. Evil? That was Lucy's word. I truly believed the evil had passed us by with the arrest of Ronald Akerman. The leaf in the teacup, if it was a scarecrow, could symbolize the one Gwendolyn was making for me.

That one was perfectly benign.

The point was that, in spite of Lucy's dire predictions, I felt certain that nothing untoward was going to happen to me or anyone tonight.

Although on past Halloweens, I hadn't been so lucky. There's something about this celebration of all things unearthly that can attract fiendish goings-on.

Don't think about scarecrows, I told myself. *Just for one night.*

"I'm going to check out the costumes," Sue said. "I'll look for your scarecrow."

So saying, she took Velvet and melted into the crowd. In truth, the crowd melted on either side of Sue, giving the Big Bad Wolf, aka Velvet, a wide berth. A chorus of *What a beautiful dog!* and *Nice dog!* followed them. Was Velvet going to find her new home tonight?

Still looking for Annica, I made my way through the milling crowd toward the buffet table. It was easy to believe Annica's fantasy had come to pass, that by some rough magic, the books on the shelves had opened to set their characters free.

I passed a diminutive Alice in Wonderland, Hester Prynne proudly wearing her scarlet 'A,' a sea captain, a robot and a man who resembled Edgar Allan Poe. Finally, I came face to face with a nurse. Cherry Ames/Leonora with a cup of cider, looking a little lost.

"Where did you disappear to?" I asked.

"I've been looking for you. I'll be glad when Jake gets here. I don't like crowds."

"Since when?"

"Since lately."

Jake intended to make a late appearance at the party with Crane.

Leonora said, "I just saw a man in a sheriff's uniform. Isn't impersonating an officer illegal?"

"I wouldn't think so. Not at a costume party. What book has a sheriff in it?"

Before she could answer, a scream pierced through the strains of eerie music. A woman's voice cried, "No, no, *no*! Get it away from me! Kill it!"

My heart began to race. *Scarecrows. Masks. Murder.* "What on earth—?"

Someone laughed. Suddenly, many people were laughing. Even Leonora seemed amused.

"Somebody must have seen Terry the Tarantula. Brent planted it in a cobweb. I saw him do it."

I could imagine the terror the woman must have felt. I would have screamed, too, and now she would feel foolish.

I said, "Is there no end to Brent's tricks? A skeleton in the fountain. A spider in the library. I'm afraid to think what else."

"It's a night for tricks," Leonora said. "Did you ever see a real tarantula, Jennet? They are huge and hairy, and they look fake."

"No, and I don't want to see any bugs. I'm going to get something to eat."

"Good idea. I will, too."

She followed me to the buffet. The cupcake supply had dwindled, their spaces filled with doughnuts. Brent's foresight was going to save the day. The baskets of fruits didn't look as if they'd been touched. Apples, pears, plums…they couldn't compete with white flour and sugar. Ask any trick-or-treater.

Leonora reached for a plum while I took my time selecting a cupcake and wishing I had a cup of tea to go with it. Earlier, I'd had tea and no cupcake.

"Did Lucy read your tea leaves yet?" I asked Leonora.

"No," she said. "I'm not sure I want to know what's in store for me."

"It's all in fun," I pointed out.

"I can see Lucy anytime. I'm going to find Miss Eidt. She may need help with the refreshments."

I should have thought of that, but then Leonora was the dessert maven, the maker of cupcakes.

What to do next?

In one corner of the library, a showing of *The Haunting of Hill House* had drawn a small audience, but I could watch a movie anytime. Elsewhere, Miss Eidt had set up a ouija board on one of the long tables. That also attracted a modest group, among them Edwina Endicott dressed as a flapper with a long rope of glittering beads.

I was tempted to join them, but decided I'd rather look at costumes and watch people. As if on cue, Scarlett O'Hara drifted into my view. She was engaged in an animated conversation with a cowboy, an older man who held a cane. She fairly sparkled. He appeared fascinated.

Good grief! Alethea had pounced on Miss Eidt's friend, Chester Mayland. Brent, I assumed, had escaped her clutches. Was no woman's man safe from that hussy's machinations?

Hoping Annica had charmed Brent away from Scarlet for good, I looked for a tall man with dark red hair but couldn't see him. Nor did I see Annica, but her Heidi costume wouldn't stand out in a crowd.

As I tossed my cupcake paper in the trash, Sue and Velvet found me again. She pushed her glasses up on her nose. "Would you help me out, Jennet?"

"Sure. What do you need?"

"Hold onto Velvet for a few minutes while I use the bathroom."

She handed me Velvet's leash. "And keep her away from the buffet."

Wagging her tail, Velvet fixed me with that look all collies know instinctively. *Take me to the buffet*, it said.

Poor dog. I hoped Sue had brought treats for her. I wished I had some, but my witch's dress didn't even have a pocket. Velvet was more than an accessory to Sue's costume. Maybe the dog had to use the bathroom, too.

"Let's go outside, Velvet," I said. "Okay?"

She didn't answer, of course, but she was willing to move. I could use a breath of fresh air. Leaving the party behind, I walked Velvet toward the door that led to the library's garden.

~ * ~

Miss Eidt's enchanted garden. How beautiful it was. I gazed in wonder at the expanse of red, orange, and russet shimmering in the strings of pumpkin lights draped on every available branch. Most of the flowers were gone, but the rain had left the earth fresh and sweet smelling.

I breathed in the air, savoring the warmth, perhaps the last of the season.

Apparently, Miss Eidt expected her guests to spill out into the garden between rain showers. She had set out wicker chairs taken from the front porch. Side tables held a mini-buffet. Cupcakes beckoned under a glass cake holder, along with a covered pitcher of cider, all providing a quiet respite for those who tired of partying.

Water splashed in the fountain, washing over the skeleton whose hands grasped the edge, as if to escape the concrete basin. I would have been seriously frightened if Sue hadn't warned me about its existence.

At the other end of the leash, Velvet stiffened. I let my hand fall on her shoulders. She felt as hard as a stone statue.

"It's okay, girl," I said. "Don't you have any business to do?"

She growled, a low menacing sound, the kind one would expect to hear from the throat of a big bad wolf, but not a gentle collie. I held tight to the leash as she lunged toward a weeping willow under which a scarecrow had been placed in a rocker.

A shiny orange shirt hid its arms from view. It had strings of yellow-orange yarn for hair and a rosy-red grin on its mask. It reminded me of Raggedy Ann. A demented version of that famous doll.

Was this the work of Brent Fowler, super prankster?

<h1 style="text-align:center">Forty-two</h1>

Apparently, Brent's contributions to Miss Eidt's Halloween party had extended beyond providing cider and extra doughnuts. A tarantula in the library, a skeleton in the pool. Just recently, I'd said, 'What else?'

This was my answer.

Still, it didn't sound like anything Brent would do. He wasn't totally insensitive. Knowing about my recent experiences, he wouldn't leave a scarecrow slouching in a chair as if it were a living person.

Why not? Halloween is a night of a thousand frights.

On the other hand, how could he know that I, or anyone for that matter, would venture into the garden on a rainy evening? And the chair under the willow tree wasn't immediately noticeable. No, something else was going on.

Velvet growled again, that wild-wolf sound rarely heard from a collie.

The scarecrow moved.

Dear God!

Shock sliced through me, forcing my heartbeat to stop. Then start again. Then stop again.

A living scarecrow?

Okay. It's one of those battery-operated toys that moves by itself.

The scarecrow straightened itself out, sat upright on the edge of the rocker...and spoke.

"Come closer, Jennet, so we can talk. I've been waiting for you. It took you long enough."

The thing removed its mask with the yarn hair attached and set it in its lap. In *her* lap.

I was looking at Tamryn Lynn. I'd never expected to see her again, certainly not in Miss Eidt's garden. Not at the party, not in a scarecrow costume.

With one hand, she smoothed her tousled hair.

Velvet continued to growl and struggled to free herself from her restraint. Her black fur bristled as if it had been electrified. I kept my hold on her leash. "It's all right, girl."

She knew I was lying. I knew it myself, but all of my instincts told me that it would be in my best interest to pretend that this was an ordinary encounter at a costume party, like any other I'd had this evening.

I tried to ignore the significance of Tamryn's other arm moving under the material of her tunic top. She was hiding something under there. A weapon?

With her free hand, she continued to fuss with her hair, a nervous gesture, I suspected.

"Tamryn," I said. "People think you disappeared, that maybe something happened to you."

"Let them think whatever they want. I don't have to account to anyone for my whereabouts."

"What do we have to talk about?"

"Things," she said. "For instance, why you blackballed me from the Rescue League after pretending to be my friend."

So that was her grievance? The decision not to admit her to the Rescue League was Sue's, although I'd concurred with it. We couldn't have Tamryn telling prospective owners she brought her dead dog back to life by scattering its ashes in her backyard.

"You told everybody I was crazy," Tamryn said. "You said I wasn't good enough to be around your precious rescues."

"I never said that."

"I think you did."

"I don't have the power to admit people to the Rescue League or to keep them out," I said.

"You were my reference. Supposedly my friend. You could have put out a good word for me."

I was silent. Arguing with a deluded person is useless as well as dangerous. Anyway, I would never bring Sue's name to Tamryn's insane attention.

"It meant a lot to me, to help rescue collies," she said. "You made that impossible."

She brought her hand out from underneath the tunic and pointed a gun at me.

A sudden calm came over me. "You're not going shoot me," I said. "You'd never get away with it. There must be a hundred people in the library."

"I can and I will. I'll be long gone by the time anyone comes to investigate.

Then she seemed to notice Velvet for the first time.

"So that's why my Cara never came back," she said. "You stole her from me."

"This isn't Cara," I said.

"I know my dog."

"Well she doesn't know you."

"Because you turned her against me. She never growled at me."

I glanced at the doorway into the library. Twenty yards or more lay between me and safety. But if Tamryn fired the gun...There was no safety for me.

Don't think about that.

"This isn't Cara," I repeated. "She's another tricolor collie. Her name is Velvet."

She didn't believe me. She took a step toward Velvet. "Cara?"

Velvet continued to growl.

Tamryn aimed the gun at her.

"I can kill her again, she said. "Now I know how to bring her back to life."

Shoot Velvet? No!

I gave the leash a mighty yank and tried to force her behind me. But Velvet had a mind of her own. She wrested the leash out of my grip and leaped on Tamryn. Fastening her teeth on Tamryn's tunic top, Velvet dragged her out of the chair to the ground.

Tamryn screamed. The gun fell from her hand and dropped down into the darkness. It fired into that same darkness, hitting no one, vanishing from my sight.

Thank God.

Velvet shook her prize as if she were an oversized stuffed doll. Tamryn's screams drowned in a roll of thunder, either from the sky or the CD. I couldn't tell; it didn't matter.

With nothing to fear now that Tamryn didn't have her gun, I had to get Velvet away from her prey before she killed her.

"Velvet! Off!"

She ignored me.

"Velvet! Leave it. Come!"

She wasn't my dog. I didn't know what commands she obeyed, if any. But Velvet didn't want to surrender her prey. She kept shaking it. Tamryn kept screaming. I tried to get my hand around Velvet's collar, but she wrenched her head out of my way. Thunder crashed again. Overhead.

I had to make Velvet listen to me.

Fine. How?

The door opened.

"Velvet!" cried Sue.

This time, Velvet listened. The horror in the screamer's voice had gotten through to her. She opened her mouth and let Tamryn fall to the ground where she lay stunned like a discarded soft toy.

Sue burst into the garden with a group of costumed revelers crowded behind her. They seemed to blur together, every color of the rainbow, a living, moving nightmare. I recognized some faces. Brent,

Miss Eidt, Edwina, Annica, Chester, Scarlett O'Hara...others. People I didn't know.

I was no longer alone in a garden with a madwoman.

In a tremulous voice, Sue said, "What happened?"

I could have been killed tonight for the stupidest reason. These people could be standing over my dead body.

"What's going on out here?" Brent demanded.

It's over. I'm safe. Velvet's safe. I'm going to be sick...

"The scarecrow," I said.

"What about it?"

I swallowed, took a deep breath, and found I could speak. "The woman in the scarecrow costume. Her name is Tamryn Lynn. She's... she had a gun."

A young man in a sheriff's costume pushed to the front of the crowd. "We heard the shot. Do you think I should make a citizen's arrest?"

"Yes, she was going to kill me. And Velvet too."

"Why?" he asked.

"Because I didn't want her to join the Rescue League."

"Come again?"

"Because she's crazy," I said.

At that Tamryn spoke, her voice hoarse from screaming. "No. She's lying. She's the one—"

Miss Eidt stepped forward to take charge. It was her party, after all.

"The woman's hurt. See all the blood? Help her up, someone, and call nine-one-one. Everybody, go back inside. Sue, take control of your dog."

Forty-three

What happened after that was anti-climactic. Paramedics transported Tamryn to the hospital, the police arrived—but not Crane—and the party continued. Back to the movie and the ouija board, and the buffet table.

Not for me, though. I was out of danger, but I couldn't stop shaking. I waited for my heartbeat to resume its normal pattern.

Maybe I was the one who should have gone to Emergency.

I recalled Edwina Endicott's big surprise. It might have been a product of her imagination, but it had come true.

Brent's CD had an endless number of fright-making sounds. Currently, we were listening to tornado sirens and winds guaranteed to make anyone's blood run cold. Even if they weren't real.

Leonora had spirited me away from the numerous people clamoring for explanations and details. In Miss Eidt's office, she made a pot of tea for all of us. It helped. So did the doughnuts Brent had brought to the party. Lucy, Annica, and Brent joined us, Brent apologetic that he hadn't been able to protect me.

"I told you to beware of Evil," Lucy reminded me.

"I never dreamed Tamryn Lynn wanted to kill me," I said. "Who could have known she felt so strongly about being denied entrance to the Rescue League?"

The office door opened, letting in a fresh wave of noise.

"Can we come in?"

It was Sue with Velvet. The little collie was wagging her tail and whining. Her wild wolf persona had vanished so thoroughly it might never have existed.

"She wants to be sure you're going to be all right," Sue said.

Velvet offered me her paw to shake. I pulled her close, kissed her soft head and ruffled her fur.

"You saved my life, Velvet. Thank you."

She eyed the doughnut. I broke off a piece for her. Small enough reward for my life.

"The way you told it a little while ago, you were the one who saved Velvet's life," Brent said.

"I tried to get her out of the line of fire, but I'm no match for an angry dog. That lunatic thought Velvet was her collie, Cara. She was going to shoot her, then bring her back to life."

Sue said, "I made the right decision not to let Tamryn in the Rescue League. I wish she'd come after me instead of you, though." She helped herself to one of the doughnuts. "It's funny. I was in the garden with Velvet admiring the lights. Then I saw the skeleton in the fountain. Where was Tamryn?"

"I didn't see a scarecrow at the party," I said. "Maybe she entered the garden through the gate. She was fixated on me. I was the one who'd kept her out of the Rescue League."

And I had never realized who my enemy was.

"It was the right decision," Sue said.

"I agree. Tamryn's grief made her lose her grip on reality. We always said she needed professional help."

"Or maybe she was always crazy," Annica said. "I wonder if she was the one who attacked you at Scarecrow House."

"She could have been. We won't know unless she confesses. Maybe she wanted to kill me then, but didn't have a gun."

"I don't understand," Brent said. "Why did she dress up like a scarecrow? How did she even know about them?"

"That may have been my doing," I said. "Tamryn was talking about decorating her yard for the fall, and I told her about the scarecrows on Mill Road. She took the idea and ran with it."

"She must have waited for the perfect moment to get you alone." Leonora shivered. "I always knew those scarecrows were up to no good."

I let that pass. Tamryn had clothed her body and her intent in a scarecrow costume. Real scarecrows, the kind Gwendolyn Larkin created, were incapable of speech or movement or plotting revenge.

I took another sip of tea and kept drinking. It helped, somewhat, to keep the residual terror at bay. "I've had enough fright for one night," I said.

And I felt that I looked like a fright, a bedraggled witch. Somewhere along the way, I'd lost my pointed hat. I was just a mortal in a black dress who wished her fingernails were pink or red. Anything but green.

I wanted Crane.

~ * ~

He came, at last, when the party was winding down. I was more than ready to go home. Jake had left with Leonora, and Miss Eidt was showing signs of tiring.

"Before you jump to conclusions, Sheriff, let me explain," Brent said.

"Explain what?"

"Why Jennet was alone. Alethea Venn distracted me. She's good at that, and Jennet disappeared with the dog."

"Tell me what happened."

"A little confrontation," Brent said.

"With Evil," Lucy added unhelpfully.

"Can anyone tell the story better?"

I could and did, making sure to emphasize the part Velvet had played. She lay at Sue's feet, the picture of collie sweetness.

"Are you sure you're all right, honey?" Crane asked.

"I'm fine. The shooter...That's another story. I only hope she survives."

"These Halloween parties are getting deadly, Miss Eidt," Crane said. "Next year, consider a smaller gathering."

"You may be right," she said, "but it was so thrilling to see all of those storybook characters wandering about the library. Oh, I almost forgot the prizes. I have to find Debbie. She took pictures. We'll have to choose the best costumes."

"And I have to take my wife home before anything else happens."

"I'm ready," I said.

He took my arm, and we left the library while Brent's CD began playing the haunting air again.

Home. As I so often reflected, it was the only place in the world that I wanted to be.

~ * ~

After that night, I realized that some key aspects of the mystery remained unaddressed. The sewing room at Scarecrow House, for example. Could Tamryn have been making her own scarecrows?

I wished I knew, but she had refused all visitors. In truth, I wouldn't have gone to see her, anyway.

Velvet had inflicted a fair amount of damage on Tamryn, enough to keep her from strenuous activity for a long while, and Tamryn had broken her leg when Velvet let her fall to the ground. Mac assured me that I didn't have to worry about her, anyway, as in all likelihood on leaving the hospital she would be admitted to a psychiatric ward.

There had been a disturbing incident at the hospital when Tamryn had grown hysterical over the visit of a golden retriever, a therapy dog. She'd tried to kill the poor creature with a knife from the kitchen.

Poor Tamryn. Finally I found it in my heart to pity her. If she had harmed Velvet, however, that would be another story.

~ * ~

Sometimes, mysteries are easily explained. They weren't bona fide mysteries to begin with.

On the day after Halloween, Gwendolyn Larkin delivered my scarecrow. She was beautiful, exactly what I'd ordered. She wore the pink gingham checked blouse with ruffles I had envisioned. Instead of a floppy flower-bedecked hat, she had a crown of gold papier mache and faux jewels. Gwendolyn named her Guinevere.

"I'm sorry I couldn't finish her for Halloween," Gwendolyn said, "but November is just beginning. You'll get a lot of use out of her."

"She's gorgeous." I placed the newcomer near our old scarecrow that looked suddenly shabby. "You do good work." Deciding to try again, I said, "Do you make them at the Mill Road House?"

"No, as I think I told you, I work at home."

"Then how can you explain the scarecrows I saw in the room at the house?"

She stared at me for a moment in exasperation, but I could tell the moment her feelings changed.

She said, "You're persistent, aren't you?"

"I guess I am. You have to be if you want to know things."

"I conduct a workshop there," she said. "Scarecrow Making One-o-one. I have five students."

"Oh."

"It's become lucrative, and it's all under the table, so please keep it to yourself."

"I will."

"Would you be interested in joining us?" she asked.

"I don't think so," I said. "Two scarecrows are enough."

Too much, in fact. Next Halloween, I'd stick with pumpkins.

Forty-four

Stripped of its decorations, the library in November appeared to hold its breath in an attitude of waiting. When I stopped by the following Saturday, dozens of boxes covered Miss Eidt's desk.

One of them lay open revealing dollhouse-sized decorations: a decorated Christmas tree, impossibly small packages, and a tiny vase filled with even tinier candy canes.

The house from the Apple Fair was there, too, wearing one of the wreaths from the dollhouse. Christmas was in the air.

Miss Eidt looked festive herself in a red knit dress, a rope of pearls, and a new shade of rose-red lipstick.

I set a box from the Hometown Bakery on the desk. "I brought breakfast," I said. "Cinnamon rolls."

"Ah, good. I gave the last of Brent's doughnuts to the birds."

"I'm glad you warmed up to the mini-scarecrow house," I said.

"I always liked it, Jennet, although I confess it made me unhappy for a while. Now I feel different."

I decided to try again as persistence had worked with Gwendolyn. "Why is that?"

Instead of answering my question, she said, "It's a sad story. Let's go in the office and I'll tell you. Bring the cinnamon rolls."

As if I'd forget.

"That house was supposed to be mine," she said. "It was purchased for me as a wedding gift."

"Scarecrow House?"

"We didn't call it that. Scarecrow House is your name for it." She filled the electric teakettle and placed the cups on the table while I cut the string on the box.

"It wasn't so gloomy in those days. I don't know who painted it that dull brown. Originally, the siding was pale yellow. It was beautiful."

She spilled loose leaves into the teapot but it seemed as if her thoughts were far away, and she had grown silent.

"Why aren't you living in it?" I asked.

"This was a long time ago, Jennet, even before I opened the library. I was engaged once, but he married someone else. It was quite unexpected, and I was devastated."

She continued her tale, continued stirring the loose tea which wasn't necessary. "After that, I went away for a while. When I came back to Foxglove Corners, I decided to turn my home into a library.

"By then, my family was gone. Ever since, I've had two homes, but the house on Mill Road was never one of them. It grew old without me. There. That's all of my past I intend to reveal."

It was indeed a sad story, but it seemed to me that she had let her sorrows go. In truth, I'd never seen her so happy.

"That man you were to have married...he was a fool."

"At the time I thought so, but I suppose it turned out for the best." She took a knife and sliced through the cinnamon rolls neatly. "Do you think one is ever too old for romance?" she asked.

"Certainly not."

Chester Maywood came to mind. And Miss Eidt's red dress. And her new lipstick and new-found glow.

"Go for it," I said.

~ * ~

The collies began to bark even before I heard the door of Crane's Jeep slam shut. They were a little more frantic than usual, sounding like a pack of wild things. Well, Crane was a match for them. As for myself, in the face of such exuberance, I'd disappear under the onslaught of paws.

He pushed the door open, but he hung back.

I looked up from the stove to see another dog prancing on the end of a leash, a tricolor collie as excited as my own collies.

"Is that Velvet?" I asked. It wasn't really a question. I would know the little tri anywhere. "Did you bring her for a visit?"

"Not exactly," he said. "I adopted her. That is, we adopted her. She's going to live with us."

"Velvet?" I murmured.

"She'll be more work, but how could we not take her? Velvet saved your life. She needs a home, and we have one. Besides, I want her. She's a little enchantress."

I couldn't believe what I was hearing. This was more like a dream than real life. I wanted Velvet, too. But I'd never told Crane. I'd scarcely admitted it to myself.

"Eight collies," I said.

"We have ten acres. You love black collies."

"I do. Okay, then. But we'd better take it slowly. They need to get used to one another."

A glance at Candy had convinced me of that. She was showing her teeth. Timid Sky had gone back under the dining room table. But Misty executed a charming play bow. The other dogs milled around the kitchen uncertain of how to react. A few tails wagged. Somebody growled.

I changed my mind. We didn't have to go slowly. I'd introduced new collies to the household before.

"Welcome, Velvet," I said. "I love you, Crane."

"I love you, too, honey, but what does that have to do with Velvet?"

"Everything."

He released her from the leash, and she touched noses with Misty. The next thing I knew the two dogs were off and running.

"No roughhousing in the house," I said.

But I didn't care. Not at all. My life was good. It was happy and was about to get better.

Meet Dorothy Bodoin

Dorothy Bodoin lives in Royal Oak, Michigan, with her blue merle collie, Layla. A graduate of Oakland University with Bachelor's and Master's degrees in English literature, Dorothy worked as a secretary for Chrysler Missile Corporation, two years of which were spent in Italy. For several years she taught English in a Michigan high school. She is the author of the Foxglove Corners Cozy Mystery series, six novels of romantic suspense, and one Gothic romance.

Other Works From The Pen Of Dorothy Bodoin

Treasure at Trail's End (Gothic romance) - The House at Trail's End seemed to beckon to Mara Marsden, promising the happy future she longed for. But could she discover its secret without forfeiting her life?

Ghost across the Water (romantic suspense) - Water falling from an invisible force and a ghostly man who appears across Spearmint Lake draw Joanna Larne into a haunting twenty-year-old mystery.

Darkness at Foxglove Corners - Foxglove Corners offers tornado survivor Jennet Greenway country peace and romance, but the secret of the yellow Victorian house across the lane holds a threat to her new life. (#1)

Winter's Tale - On her first winter in Foxglove Corners Jennet Greenway battles dognappers, investigates the murder of the town's beloved veterinarian, and tries to outwit a dangerous enemy. (#3)

A Shortcut through the Shadows - Jennet Greenway's search for the missing owner of her rescue collie, Winter, sets her on a collision course with an unknown killer. (#4)

Cry for the Fox - In Foxglove Corners, the fox runs from the hunters, the animal activists target the Hunt Club, and a killer stalks human prey on the fox trail. (#2)

The Witches of Foxglove Corners - With a haunting in the library, a demented prankster who invades her home, and a murder in Foxglove Corners, Halloween turns deadly for Jennet Greenway. (#5)

The Snow Dogs of Lost Lake - A ghostly white collie and a lost locket lead Jennet Greenway to a body in the woods and a dangerous new mystery. (#6)

The Collie Connection - As Jennet Greenway's wedding to Crane Ferguson approaches, her happiness is shattered when a Good Samaritan deed leaves her without her beloved black collie, Halley, and ultimately in grave danger. (#7)

A Time of Storms - When a stranger threatens her collie and she hears a cry for help in a vacant house, Jennet Ferguson suspects that her first summer as a wife may be tumultuous. (#8)

The Dog from the Sky - Jennet's life takes a dangerous turn when she rescues an abused collie. Soon afterward, a girl vanishes without a trace. Ironically she had also rescued an abused collie. Is there a connection between the two incidents? (#9)

Spirit of the Season - Mystery mixes with holiday cheer as a phantom ice skater returns to the lake where she died, and a collie is accused of plotting her owner's fatal accident. (#10)

Another Part of the Forest - Danger rides the air when a kidnapper whisks his victims away in a hot air balloon, and a false friend puts a curses on a collie breeder's first litter. (#11)

Where Have All the Dogs Gone? - An animal activist frees the shelter dogs in and around Foxglove Corners to save them from being destroyed. Running wild in the countryside, they face an equally distressing fate and post a risk to those who come in contact with them. (#12)

The Secret Room of Eidt House - A rabid dog that should have died months ago from the dread disease runs free in the woods of Foxglove Corners, and the library's long-kept secret unleashes a series of other strange events. (#13)

Follow a Shadow - A shadowy intruder haunts Jennet's woods by night, and a woman who can't accept the death of her collie asks Jennet to help her find Rainbow Bridge where she believes her dog waits for her. (#14)

The Snow Queen's Collie - A white collie puppy appears on the porch of the Ferguson farmhouse during a Christmas Eve snowstorm. In another part of Foxglove Corners a collie breeder's show prospect disappears. Meanwhile, the painting Jennet's sister gave her for Christmas begins to exhibit strange qualities. (#15)

The Door in the Fog - A wounded dog disappears in the fog. A blue door on the side of a barn vanishes. Strange wildflowers and a sound of weeping haunt a meadow. The woods keep their secret, and a curse refuses to die. (#16)

Dreams and Bones - At Brent Fowler's newly purchased Spirit Lamp Inn, a renovation turns up human bones buried in the inn's backyard, rekindling interest in the case of a young woman who disappeared from the inn several decades ago. As Jennet tries to solve this mystery, she doesn't realize it may be her last. (#17)

A Ghost of Gunfire - Months after gunfire erupted in her classroom at Marston High School, leaving one student dead and one seriously wounded, Jennet begins to hear a sound of gunshots inaudible to anyone else. Meanwhile, she resolves to find the demented person who is tying dogs to trees and leaving them to die. (#18)

The Silver Sleigh - Rosalyn Everett was missing and presumed dead. Her collies had been rescued, and her house was abandoned. But a blue merle collie haunts her woods and a figure in bridal white traverses the property. (#19)

The Stone Collie - Jennet's discovery of a collie puppy chained in the yard of a vacant house sets her on a search for a man whose activities may threaten Foxglove Corners' security. Meanwhile, horror story novelist Lucy Hazen is mystified when scenes from her work-in-progress are duplicated in real life. (#20)

The Mists of Huron Court - The house was beautiful, a vintage pink Victorian in a picturesque but lonely country setting, and the girl playing ball with her dog in the yard was friendly, suggesting that she and Jennet walk their dogs together some time. Jennet thinks she has made a new friend until she returns to the house and finds a tumbling down ruin where the Victorian once stood and no sign that the girl and dog have ever been there. ((#21)

Down a Dark Path - What hold does the pink Victorian on Huron Court have on Brent Fowler who is determined to re-create the home of long-dead Violet Randall? When he disappears, could he have been cast adrift in time? (#22))

Shadow of the Ghost Dog - An invisible dog grieves inside the house chosen as a setting for the movie based on Lucy Hazen's book *Devilwish*, and a landscaper unearths a human skeleton in the backyard while planting shrubs. (#23))

The Dark Beyond the Bridge - The discovery of a secret ghost town in a densely rural area of Michigan's lower peninsula leads to mystery and danger for Jennet Ferguson and her friends. (#24)

The Deadly Fields of Autumn - An antique television set that airs an obscure Western at random times and a woman who disappears with her newly-adopted rescue dog draw Jennet into a puzzling mystery. (#25)

The Lost Collies of Silverhedge - Collie breeder Madselin Rivard was dead, leaving her prized, valuable collies uncared for in their kennel. Jennet and her friends rescue five of them, but eight remain unaccounted for. (#26)

All the Pretty Little Collies - Danger stalks the collies of Foxglove Corners when an unknown villain begins tossing poisoned meat into their yards, and a girl with a winning blue merle collie is warned via threatening messages to withdraw her dog from competition or risk the consequences. (#27)

Phantom in the Pond - Brent Fowler's plan to open a house for geriatric collies goes awry when strange things begin to happen in his newly-purchased country estate. (#28)

Letter to Our Readers

Enjoy this book?

You can make a difference

As an independent publisher, Wings ePress, Inc. does not have the financial clout of the large New York Publishers. We can't afford large magazine spreads or subway posters to tell people about our quality books.

But, we do have something much more effective and powerful than ads. We have a large base of loyal readers.

Honest Reviews help bring the attention of new readers to our books.

If you enjoyed this book, we would appreciate it if you would spend a few minutes posting a review on the site where you purchased this book or on the Wings ePress, Inc. webpages at: https://wingsepress.com/

Visit Our Website

For The Full Inventory
Of Quality Books:

Wings ePress.Inc
https://wingsepress.com/

Quality trade paperbacks and downloads
in multiple formats,
in genres ranging from light romantic comedy
to general fiction and horror.
Wings has something for every reader's taste.
Visit the website, then bookmark it.
We add new titles each month!

Wings ePress Inc.

3000 N. Rock Road

Newton, KS 67114